Horses and Friends Series

A Horse for Kate
Silver Spurs
Mystery Rider
Blue Ribbon Trail Ride (Spring 2016)

MIRALEE FERRELL

Mystery
Rider

David C Cook®

transforming lives together

MYSTERY RIDER
Published by David C Cook
4050 Lee Vance View
Colorado Springs, CO 80918 U.S.A.

David C Cook Distribution Canada
55 Woodslee Avenue, Paris, Ontario, Canada N3L 3E5

David C Cook U.K., Kingsway Communications
Eastbourne, East Sussex BN23 6NT, England

The graphic circle C logo is a registered trademark of David C Cook.

This story is a work of fiction. Characters and events are
the product of the author's imagination. Any resemblance
to any person, living or dead, is coincidental.

LCCN 2015933704
ISBN 978-1-4347-0737-6
eISBN 978-0-7814-1361-9

© 2015 Miralee Ferrell
Published in association with Tamela Hancock Murray of The Steve
Laube Agency, 5025 N. Central Ave., #635, Phoenix, AZ 85012

The Team: Ingrid Beck, Ramona Cramer Tucker, Nick Lee,
Amy Konyndyk, Tiffany Thomas, Karen Athen
Cover Design: DogEared Design, Kirk DouPonce

Printed in the United States of America
First Edition 2015

1 2 3 4 5 6 7 8 9 10

062915

To Kate, my darling granddaughter.
I hope by the time you're old enough
to read these books, you'll love horses
and reading as much as I do.

Chapter One

Upper Hood River Valley, Odell, Oregon
Summer, Present Day

Kate Ferris sprawled on the grass next to the newly painted paddock fence on her parents' farm. "Thanks for your help, guys. It sure goes faster with more than one person working." She shot a sideways glance at Melissa Tolbert, still barely able to believe the girl who had always been so snotty at school had shown up and offered to help. "You're not bad at slapping on paint."

Melissa leaned back on her elbows and grinned. "Even if Colt didn't keep his word to not splatter me with it."

Freckle-faced Colt Turner removed a long piece of straw from between his lips. "Hey, you said not to make you look like the rest of us, but I didn't make any promises."

Tori Velasquez, Kate's best friend, rolled her eyes. "We should get the brushes cleaned and the rest of the paint closed up and put away before you two start fighting again."

"Not fighting." Melissa arched one blonde brow. "Just discussing."

"Whatever." Tori smiled. "I was kinda wondering …" She eyed Melissa.

"Yeah?"

"Well, I never got to see those spurs you won while showing Capri. I don't suppose you've got them in your back pocket or anything."

Kate snorted a laugh. "Now that would be funny—no, not funny, painful. Melissa wouldn't dare sit if she did. Could you bring them over sometime so we can all see them?" Pivoting toward Melissa, Kate was surprised at the girl's suddenly serious expression. "Of course, you don't have to. It's not a big deal." The last thing Kate wanted was for the recent truce between Melissa, herself, and her two best friends to be ruined.

Melissa turned away for a minute, then back. "I'll do better than that. They really should be yours—or at least belong to the barn, since it was your horse I rode, Kate. How about I bring them over and give them to you?" she asked, her face earnest.

Kate shook her head, her long brown braids swinging. "No way! Mom and Dad would never agree, and I don't either. You won those spurs fair and square. You gave me the blue ribbon to put on Capri's stall door, and that's good enough. If you hadn't been such a good rider, Capri wouldn't have won the championship. There's no way I'd have made her jump that well."

Spots of pink appeared on Melissa's cheeks, and she ducked her head. "Okay. Thanks." She raised her eyes and stared at each of them in turn. "So, are you guys entering the Fort Dalles parade this summer?"

"Huh?" Kate lifted one brow. "I only moved here in March. I'm not sure I know what or where that is."

Tori poked Kate in the side with her elbow. "Up the river at The Dalles, silly. The rodeo and parade are for Fort Dalles Days, 'cause that's what the town was at first—a fort, way over a hundred years ago. It's pretty cool. They have a carnival, rodeo, parade, and other stuff, and it lasts a week or so." She turned to Melissa. "But why would any of us want to enter the parade?"

Colt sat up straight, and his blue eyes brightened. "The barn. Right, Melissa? You're thinking Kate and her parents should do something in the parade to advertise the boarding stable here?"

Melissa shrugged. "Yeah, why not?"

Kate wrapped one of her braids around her finger. "It's way too hard and expensive to build a float."

Melissa nodded. "Right. But how about riding your horses and making banners to put over their hindquarters, behind their saddles? You could even dress them or yourselves up if you wanted to. Cowgirls"—she shot Colt a look—"or cowboys … or just wear your English riding gear, and Colt can be the cowboy. It doesn't matter so much what you wear, but I think it's a good idea to be in the parade. It's a cheap way to let people know you're open for business."

"I like it!" Kate gazed at each of her friends. "So, are you guys in? Do you want to ride your horses in the parade and help us advertise the barn?"

Tori's dark-brown eyes widened, and she pulled back. "I don't know, Kate. What if my horse gets scared at all the noise, and I can't handle him? I'm not an expert rider like Melissa, or even as good as you or Colt."

Melissa waved her fingers. "Hey, I wasn't trying to push in. I only suggested it for you guys. You don't need to include me."

Kate tipped her head. "You aren't getting out of it that easy, Melissa Tolbert. This was your idea, so you're stuck with us, since you seem to know so much about what we're supposed to do."

A shrill tone sounded in Melissa's pocket, and she took out a cell phone. "Sorry, guys. My mom. I'll be right back." She pushed to her feet and walked a few yards away, keeping her back to the group. Her voice dropped, but a light breeze pushed her words toward Kate and her friends. "Yeah. Just hanging out with those kids from the barn. No big deal. I can leave if you don't want me here."

Colt leaned forward and whispered to Kate and Tori, "Her mom was pretty pushy about her earning the most points at the horse show. I wonder if she'll want Melissa helping us. We're not exactly rich or anything. She might not want to hang around." He contorted his face into one of his trademark comical expressions.

Kate laughed. "I wondered that too." She sobered. "And to be honest, whether this *new* Melissa will last. From what she said to her mom, it doesn't sound like being here is a big deal to her. I want to trust her, but after the way she treated us at school and then bossed us around when she came to the barn, I'm not sure I can."

"I think we need to be nice to her," dark-haired Tori replied. "She didn't have to help with the fence or give us suggestions for the parade. How about inviting her to our sleepover tonight? We could start planning what we want to do for the parade."

"I think that's pushing things too fast," Kate said. "I agree with Colt. We're not in Melissa's circle of friends, and I doubt she'd even want to come. How about we ask if she wants to be part of our parade group and nothing more for now?"

Someone's throat cleared behind the group, and they all turned. Melissa stood, frowning, several feet away. "Are you talking about me?"

"Sorry, Melissa. We were talking about the parade and wondering if you'd want to help." Tori paused. "We were thinking Colt could be in charge, since he's the only guy."

Colt raised his hands and laughed. "No way. I'm no organizer, but I'm guessing Melissa would be good at that kind of thing. I vote for Melissa."

Tori clapped. "I second it!"

Kate nodded. "It's decided. Melissa's the head of our parade committee, if she agrees." She exchanged glances with Tori. She knew what her kindhearted friend was thinking. They needed to invite Melissa to come tonight. It was the right thing to do. But Kate bet they'd end up being sorry.

"Seriously? You guys want me to help?" Melissa, seemingly rooted to the ground, gazed around the small semicircle.

"Yep." Kate smiled. "But don't take it as too big a compliment. You might end up being sorry you ever agreed. If you'll do it, and our parents agree, then you're it."

The uncertainty in Melissa's green eyes turned to acceptance, and a hint of joy seemed to shine through. "Right. So when do you want to start planning?"

Kate and Tori looked at each other. Colt was coming to the party for popcorn and a movie, then planned to go home while the two girls stayed up in Kate's room talking and giggling. Did Kate really want to include Melissa in their private party when she'd been such a pain in the past, dissing them and being so condescending? Tori gave a tiny nod. Kate sneaked a glance at Colt, who barely shrugged one shoulder.

Melissa searched Kate's face. "What's up? Am I missing something?"

"Nope. You're not going to miss a thing. In fact, if you're free tonight, we'll start planning after we eat a big bowl of popcorn. You wanna come to my house tonight?"

Melissa stared at Kate as if stunned. "With all of you?"

"Yeah. Me, Tori, and Colt. We were going to have a sleepover, but I don't know if you'd want to do that."

Colt nearly choked on his straw and blew it out of his mouth. "Hey, now. You're going to ruin my reputation. I am *not* staying for the sleepover. Just the food and a movie— unless we change it to food and talking about the parade. Got it?"

Kate giggled. "Like my parents would allow a guy to stay the night, or like we'd want you to." She wrinkled her nose. "No offense, Colt, but your socks stink when you take your shoes off, and no matter how nice you are, we don't want any guys crashing our girl time."

"Good!" Colt heaved a huge sigh. "You had me scared for a minute there. But I'm in for popcorn and planning, if everyone else wants to do that."

Melissa nodded slowly. "Okay. I know my mom won't care. I'll come for the popcorn and to talk about the parade, but I don't think I can stay long—not for the sleepover anyway. I've got something else I need to do tonight … and honestly, I'm not sure you guys would want me around that long."

Kate jumped in. "We didn't say that, Melissa. I wasn't sure you'd feel comfortable hanging out with us for a longer time—you know, after all that's happened in the past. But you can if you'd like. Really."

"Thanks …" Melissa hesitated. "But not this time. I really am busy later tonight."

A small smile flickered across her lips, as if she had a secret she wasn't telling. Kate winced inwardly. She'd seen that same expression before when Melissa was scheming something that wouldn't be fun for the rest of them. She and Tori had been on the receiving end of the wealthy girl's meanness too many times. As for Colt, he seemed to ride above all the ruckus, not letting any of it bother him.

Did I make the wrong decision inviting her? Kate now wished she hadn't. Sure, Melissa had come over and helped paint the fence, and she seemed genuinely sorry for the snobby way she'd treated them before. *Being nice for a day or two is one thing*, Kate thought. *But sometimes people don't change, even if you think they have.*

The last thing Kate wanted was to bring more trouble into her own life, much less Tori's or Colt's. They had enough to do with getting the Ferris family's horse barn up and running with paying customers.

Kate settled into the couch with a bowl of popcorn and grinned at her friends, excited they'd made the decision to come and talk about the parade. Her mom and dad had said they'd consider allowing them to ride in the parade after they heard what ideas Kate, Tori, Colt, and Melissa came up with, so at least they hadn't said no first thing.

Kate clicked the remote and turned off the TV. "That was a good movie, but we'd better get back to planning. Melissa, you're in charge, so you should take over."

Melissa's blonde curls bounced with excitement. "I've been thinking about it all day. First, we need to make banners to drape behind our saddles with the barn name. Second, we need to come up with colorful costumes we can wear, or our horses can wear—something that will draw attention. We could wear our riding outfits, but will anyone really notice us if we do? Isn't that too"—she made air quotes—"*normal?*"

Colt slumped back against the couch. "I hope you don't mean doing something dumb like dressing up as *Arabian Nights* or fairy-tale characters. That would not be cool. I don't see why I can't be a cowboy riding a horse. After all, it is a parade for the Fort Dalles Rodeo."

"I get your point, Colt," Tori added. "But Melissa might be right. Lots of people ride horses in parades—the rodeo princesses and clubs—and pretty soon you hardly notice them. Maybe we do need something a little different to stand out."

"But where would we get costumes, and how would we pay for them? And what kind of banners would we make?" Kate pondered a minute. "Paper would rip too easily, and I'm no good at sewing. I've seen horses with silk banners and professional lettering, but we can't afford that. It's a great idea, but we have to make sure that whatever we decide will work."

"I see what you mean," Melissa said. "Our regular riding gear would be cheap and easy, but do we really want to look cheap?" She tossed her head. "I sure don't."

Tori sighed and shot a glance at Kate. "Maybe we could think of a way to earn money for nice banners or costumes. I agree that we need something that catches people's attention."

Colt nodded. "That might work. If you girls want to do a bunch of baking, we could have a bake sale."

Kate raised her brows. "And what would the boy be doing while the girls are baking?"

Colt smirked. "Licking the bowl and doing quality control on the goodies."

Tori smacked his arm. "More like washing the dishes and doing publicity."

Melissa gazed from one to the other, her mouth agape. "Are you guys like this all the time?"

Kate snickered. "Pretty much. We can be serious when we have to be though." She probably should say she was sorry, but after Melissa's stuck-up comment about not looking cheap, the words would have choked her. Apparently some of the old Melissa was still hanging around. "Let's get back to business. Colt suggested a bake sale. What else?"

"A car wash?" Melissa offered.

"Or maybe some kind of raffle," Tori added.

Kate set her soda glass on the table. "That might work. I could talk to Mom about raffling off a riding lesson."

"But you'd have to pay the trainer for the lesson, right? Would it be worth it?" Melissa asked.

"If enough people bought a ticket, we'd raise more than the lesson cost. But it might not be the best prize. We probably need to think about that a little longer." Kate leaned against the couch.

Colt drummed his fingers on the coffee table. "Yeah. Having a good prize would get a lot more buyers."

At that moment Kate's attention was drawn to a slight figure in the doorway to the hall leading upstairs. Her little brother, Pete, stood there, clutching his blanket. He shuffled his feet toward her.

Kate jumped up. "Pete. Why aren't you in bed? Are you looking for Mom? She's in the TV room with Dad."

He didn't respond and kept his eyes averted.

She walked across the room. "What's the matter, little guy? Can't sleep again?"

He hunched one shoulder.

Kate knew better than to draw him into a hug like she wanted to do. Her six-year-old, autistic brother didn't like to be touched unless it was his idea. "Want me to take you back to your room and tuck you in?"

"Want a drink of water."

Melissa suddenly appeared at Pete's side and touched his brown hair, but he didn't pull back. "I can get it for you, buddy."

Kate glanced at the girl, then at her brother. It had amazed her the first time she'd seen this soft side of Melissa with her brother, and it still had the ability to surprise her. Not that she wasn't glad. Melissa could as easily have been mean to Pete. So many people didn't understand kids with problems. "Thanks, Melissa. But I'll take him."

Melissa gave a short nod. "Okay." She headed back to the couch and sank into the cushions.

"Pete?" Kate's mom stepped into the room. "There you are. Come on, honey, let's go." She extended her hand, and Pete moved to her side but didn't reach out to her. "You kids go ahead with your planning, and I'll get this little guy back to bed." She touched Pete on his back and urged him toward the hallway.

Kate called after them, "He wants water, Mom."

"I'll take care of it. Thanks, Kate." Mom disappeared around the corner.

Silence fell over the group. Then Melissa got up. "I'd better go. Mom said she'd be waiting outside at seven thirty, and it's twenty-five after now. Thanks for inviting me. I hope you have fun the rest of the night." She smirked slightly.

"Bye, Melissa," their voices chorused as Melissa headed out the door.

"Keep thinking of ideas," Kate called after her.

Colt grabbed the remote. "Want to watch a scary movie?"

Tori groaned. "I hate scary movies. They scare me."

"That's the idea, silly."

Kate elbowed him. "We don't even own any scary movies. What did you guys think about Melissa?"

Tori sobered. "What do you mean?"

"I don't know. She was helpful and everything, but she seemed … odd somehow. I can't explain it."

Colt rolled his eyes. "You're imagining things, Kate. If anything, she's more normal than we are." He grinned.

Tori huffed. "Colt, sometimes I want to smack you."

He shrank away as though scared but grinned again, wider.

"Seriously, I didn't notice anything weird about her," Tori reasoned. "Except for the comment about not looking cheap, but that didn't really surprise me. Maybe she was worried she wouldn't fit in. We're not exactly the crowd she runs with, you know."

Kate thought for a moment. "Well, it kinda bugged me. I guess it's still hard for me to believe she wants to be our friend after the way she acted toward us for so long."

Colt kicked off his shoes, leaned into the couch, and planted his heels on the coffee table. "Ah, she's all right. I don't think she's a Christian, though. I guess it's up to us to do the right thing and make her feel welcome."

Kate hesitated. "I just don't want to get burned. Know what I mean?" Melissa seemed decent enough now, but was she only playing a game, maybe because she was bored? Would she then go back to her old self?

The other two were quiet, as if thinking.

Finally Tori announced, "But we should give her a chance, right?"

"Right," Colt said swiftly.

Kate chimed in with her agreement a bit more slowly. "I wonder what else she had to do tonight. A little late to be heading to another friend's house, and with school out, there's no homework."

Colt drew in a deep breath and blew it out, his eyes closing. "If you don't want to watch another movie, maybe I'll take a little nap."

Kate waved a hand in front of her face. "Remember what we said about your stinky socks? We weren't kidding!" She placed her foot next to his ankle and pushed. "Ugh. Boys are gross."

Colt sat up. "Aww! You've stuck a knife right through my heart." He chuckled. "I probably should head home too. Mind if I use your phone and give Mom a call?"

"Go ahead. You know where it is. You sure you don't want any more popcorn first?"

"Not me." The answers came in unison from Colt and Tori.

Colt's long stride took him out of the room in a couple of seconds, but a short time later he hollered over his shoulder, "Hey, come see this. Weird, if you ask me."

Kate bolted into the kitchen first, with Tori on her heels, and said, "What's up?"

Colt moved to the sliding glass door and pointed. "A black horse. That's not a big deal, but the rider looks strange."

Tori crept up beside him. "The horse is gorgeous!"

Colt grunted assent. "But what's the deal with the person riding him? You can't tell if it's a man or a woman, and it's awful warm to be wearing a full slicker with a hood."

Kate shaded her eyes against the glass. "I wish it wasn't dusk, so we could see the rider better. Look, they're trotting now and moving on up the road. I think the rider's a woman or a teenager. Doesn't look big enough to be a man, and she's all hunched over the horse's mane. Do you think she's sick or something?"

Colt slid the door open. "Maybe we should make sure the rider is okay."

Kate and Tori slipped outside, with Colt following. He nudged Kate in the side. "You going to holler or just stand there?"

Kate made a face at him but took a few steps toward the gravel road that ran behind her house. "Hey," she called toward the horse and rider, "are you all right?"

The horse slowed for a second. Then the rider bumped him in the side and they took off at a fast trot.

Tori stepped up beside Kate. "That was rude. She had to have heard you, but then she ignored you."

Kate nodded. "It's a mystery. I've never seen that horse before, but maybe we should ask around and see what we can find out. It sure seemed like the rider had something to hide." She faced Tori and Colt. "The person was the same size as Melissa. You don't suppose that's why she had to hurry home? But why wouldn't she stop and show us her new horse?"

Colt scrunched his brow. "It doesn't make a bit of sense. I say we keep a close eye out tomorrow night in case the rider comes back. What if she stole that horse?"

Chapter Two

Kate, Tori, and Colt sat in Kate's backyard for the third night in a row, but they still hadn't seen the mysterious horse and rider again. Kate's parents didn't mind them keeping an eye out for the new horse in the neighborhood. However, none of the trio thought it was a good idea to share their suspicions with Mr. and Mrs. Ferris that the rider could have been Melissa.

Tori settled back in a lawn chair. "I feel kinda stupid. There's no reason for Melissa to ride a new horse past your house right before dark. I don't know why we ever thought it was her to begin with."

Colt plucked a long blade of grass from where he lay stretched out on the lawn and stuck it between his teeth. "Me too. It's not like she threw eggs at the house or anything."

Kate had struggled with some of the same feelings for the past couple of days. "I'm the one who started us thinking that way … all because she smirked before she left. Lame, huh?"

Tori stared at her. "Seriously? Melissa smirks at stuff all the time. That's nothing new. I figured she'd done more than that."

Kate shifted in her chair, feeling silly. "Well, she's hatched little schemes in the past that were aimed at us. She didn't act like she wanted to hang out with us when we said she could, and she didn't explain what else she had to do that night, so I guess …" All of a sudden the words sounded even more lame than what she'd said earlier. "And when her mom called the other day, it sounded like Melissa thought we weren't important, and that she was ready to leave anytime."

Colt smacked his leg. "I know. What do you say we flat out ask her what's up? It's not like we've heard from her again, and she's supposed to be the head of our parade committee. Instead of talking about her, maybe we should be up-front about it and give her a chance to explain."

"Good idea, Colt. I'm embarrassed now that we thought all that stuff about her." Tori peeked at Kate. "Although I have to admit, she hasn't been the nicest or easiest person to be around in the past, so I get why Kate would be suspicious."

Kate expelled a sigh. "Thanks for trying to make me feel better, but I messed up and I know it. I'll call her now." She swung her legs over the side of the lawn chair and started to stand. "Wait a second. Do you hear that?"

Colt rolled over onto his side in the grass. "Nope. What?"

"Shh." Kate held her finger to her lips. "Hoofbeats. Coming this way from the same direction as the other night."

Colt and Tori bounded to their feet, with Kate close on their heels.

Colt tiptoed toward the road but kept behind a fir tree. "Come on. You girls want to see, or what?"

Now that the rider had returned, Kate was suddenly scared. What if it was Melissa, and she didn't answer? Or what if she thought they were spying on her and never spoke to them again? Not that it would be a huge loss. They'd never been friends and had only formed a truce of sorts at the horse show last weekend. But the idea of turning Melissa into an enemy again made Kate sick to her stomach.

She grabbed Tori's hand. "Maybe this isn't such a good idea."

"Huh?" Tori blinked rapidly. "It's not like we're doing anything bad. We only want to see who it is, right?"

"I suppose." Kate allowed Tori to tug her toward the fir tree with overhanging branches. "At least it's almost dark again, so she's not likely to see us hiding here."

Colt didn't reply but stepped out from behind the trunk as the rider came opposite the yard. "Hey, that's a nice horse. What's its name? Can you stop so we can see him?"

The rider pivoted their direction, obviously startled. Kate could barely make out a wrinkled face under the hood drawn over the head. A breeze wafted, and a long strand of white hair escaped the hood and danced in front of the rider's face.

Definitely not Melissa.

Relieved, Kate called loudly, "Do you live around here?"

Instantly the rider touched the horse's side with a heel, sending it into a fast canter. Rocks from the gravel road kicked up behind as the pair disappeared down the road.

Tori groaned from behind the tree. "That went well. Sheesh. Either that person has something to hide or is scared of kids. Don't know which. But at least it's not Melissa. I'm glad about that."

Kate nodded. "Did you see the white hair and wrinkled face? Creepy, if you ask me. I still couldn't tell if it's a man or a woman. Could you, guys?"

Colt shook his head. "I think it might be a woman because of the size, but some men are really small too, so who knows? I hate to keep saying *she or they*. If we're going to try to figure this out, we ought to call him or her the Mystery Rider from now on."

"Cool. The Mystery Rider." Kate grinned and slapped her palms together. "Now all we have to do is solve the mystery."

The next day, Kate leaned her hip against a cupboard in the kitchen. "Mom, do you think I should call Melissa? It's so weird that she hasn't come over or called since we first talked about the parade. Tori and I wonder if she's lost interest and ditched us."

Her mother slid the rack into the dishwasher and shut the door, then faced Kate. "Could something have upset her?"

Kate reflected for a moment. "I don't think so. She overheard us talking about her and the parade in the afternoon, but we explained we wanted her to be part of it and even be in charge."

Mom's eyebrows went up. "Is that all you were saying?"

"Yeah … well, at least right then."

Her mom's eyes narrowed like they always did when she was trying to extract the truth. "And what does that mean? What aren't you telling me?"

Kate knew that look and that she might as well give her mother some answers now. "Melissa came by and helped us paint the rest of the fence. Her phone rang, and she stepped away for a bit, so Tori, Colt, and I were talking."

"About Melissa?"

"Kinda … I guess." Kate shifted uncomfortably.

"Either you were or you weren't, Kate."

"Okay, we were," Kate admitted. "But nothing bad. She told her mom she was hanging out with us, but she didn't seem to care whether she stayed or not. I guess that made me feel weird. We were talking about asking her to take part in our parade planning, and then Tori said we should invite her to spend the night. I said that might not be a great idea, 'cause Melissa's never been part of our group and runs with another crowd." She added defensively, "It's not like she was acting all excited to be with us anyway, and Tori, Colt, and I already had the night planned."

"Then what happened?" Mom settled into a chair by the kitchen table.

"Melissa walked up and asked if we were talking about her."

"Uh-huh. And what did you say?"

"That we were, and we wanted her to come over that night to talk about the parade and wondered if she wanted to spend the night." Kate wished Mom didn't always know when some-thing was bugging her.

Her mother studied her. "But you didn't really mean it, right? You were hoping she'd say no."

"Only to the overnight part. I didn't care if she came over and ate popcorn and talked about the parade." Kate intertwined her fingers. "But honestly, Mom, I didn't think she'd fit in with me and Tori at a sleepover. Besides, she said no, so it doesn't matter, right?"

"You tell me, Kate. What if you'd been Melissa and heard other kids talking about you. Would you want to spend the night with them and take the chance of feeling left out or ignored?"

Kate huffed. "We didn't ignore her when she came over. We'd already put her in charge. Besides, it's not like she's been supernice to any of us since she brought her horse to our barn."

Mom leveled a stern look at Kate. "So it's okay to get even with someone if she wasn't kind to you in the past? It doesn't matter if you hurt someone's feelings … Is that what you're saying?"

Kate wavered between irritation and guilt. Her mother was right, but she hated to admit it. She'd been feeling bad from the moment she realized Melissa might have overheard part of what she'd said that afternoon. But she and her friends had done a good job covering it, and Melissa seemed happy enough when she'd come to the Ferris house. "No, it's not okay, and I wasn't trying to get even. I just didn't think she'd fit in, that's all."

Mom smiled. "Good. I wanted you to think about how Melissa felt. Have you tried calling her? It might be a good idea to reach out, in case she's worried you kids don't really want her around. You could tell her about the black horse you saw and see if she knows who owns it."

Relief flooded Kate. Mom wasn't mad at her, and she understood. "Great idea. I'll do that now. Maybe I'll see if she wants to come over this afternoon and walk with me and Tori and Colt. We'll go up the road in the direction the rider headed and see if we can spot the horse in a pasture. If you and Dad don't care, that is."

Mom nodded. "That sounds like a great idea, and a walk might be fun. But you have to finish your chores before you go, and I'd like you to read a story to Pete while I get some work done."

"Sure, Mom. I'll read him two or three if you want. Is he taking a nap now?"

"Yes, but he'll be up soon. You know the four of you could take your bikes and cover a little more area, as long as you aren't gone all afternoon. Who knows? You might even uncover the mystery today." Mom's eyes twinkled.

"Colt thinks the horse might be stolen." Kate blurted out the words without thinking, then placed her fingers over her lips.

Her mother frowned. "What gives him that idea?"

"I don't know. I guess because the person riding the horse looks like she's trying to hide her appearance, and she only takes him out close to dark. Maybe she needs to ride him and get him ready to sell, so she only takes him on back roads where there isn't much traffic and not as many people are likely to see him ..." Kate's flow of words trailed off when she saw her mom's doubtful expression. "You never know, Mom. There could be a horse-stealing ring in our area. We'd better start locking the doors on the barn at night. I don't want someone sneaking in and taking Capri."

Chapter Three

Kate, Tori, Colt, and Melissa straddled their bikes in Kate's backyard. They'd filled Melissa in on the Mystery Rider as soon as she'd arrived, and Kate hadn't questioned Melissa about why they hadn't heard from her. Kate had an uneasy feeling her mother was right—that Melissa had overheard something.

Colt rocked his bike back and forth. "You girls ready to go, or are you going to stand around and gab all day? And are we going the same direction, or do we split up?"

Kate rushed to answer. "I say we stay together. We won't cover as much area, but if we split up, Melissa is the only one with a cell phone. Plus, one person can keep an eye on any traffic while the others check out pastures and back lots. Sound okay?"

"Sure." All three of her friends chorused the answer.

Colt pushed off first. "If you girls want to look for the horse, I'll lead and watch for traffic."

Melissa pulled up beside Kate as they pedaled across the backyard. "How are we going to spot him? Does he have any markings that make him stand out?"

Tori's voice drifted forward. "He's all black with a small white star on his forehead and gorgeous. I haven't seen another horse like him in Odell."

Melissa nodded and kept pace with Kate. "What do you plan to do if you find him?"

Kate instantly grabbed her brakes.

Tori squealed. "Hey, I almost ran into you! What's up?"

"Sorry," Kate said. "Hey, Colt. Slow up, will you?"

He stopped on the edge of the road and looked back. "Problem?"

"Yeah." Kate coasted to a stop behind him and waited for Melissa and Tori to do the same. "Melissa asked a really good question. What do we do if we find the horse?"

"Sheesh." Colt swiped his fingers across the top of his head. "Why didn't any of us think of that? Good call, Melissa. That's why we made you the head of the parade committee."

Tori grinned. "Yeah. And my parents finally said it's okay with them if I ride in the parade, as long as an adult is present."

"Cool! I asked my mom if she'd ride with us, and she's thinking about it," Kate said. "But back to our Mystery Rider. What about if we spot the horse? Do we go up and knock on the door and ask the owner what she's doing riding at night with a long, hooded slicker?"

Melissa groaned. "Seriously?"

Kate's muscles tensed at Melissa's snippy tone. It felt like how Melissa had been before the horse show. "And why not?" Kate couldn't help her tiny scowl.

Melissa rolled her eyes. "Remember? You told me Colt was worried the woman might have stolen the horse. If she's a criminal, she could lock us in her house and keep us there. I say we scope out the area, then decide what to do." She looked at Kate and bit her lip. "Sorry. I didn't mean to say it that way."

A breath whooshed out of Kate, and she grinned. "No big deal. I like your idea. Let's do it." She jumped back on her bike and started pedaling. "Now who's standing around, Colt?"

He mounted his bike and raced past her as if she were standing still. Tori drew alongside Kate and giggled. "Boys."

"Yeah." Kate tossed a glance over her shoulder at Melissa. "Hey, there's nobody coming. Want to come up here with us?"

There was a slight pause, then, "Naw. I'm good. If a car comes down the road very fast, we might not get out of the way in time. Besides, I'm watching for that horse."

"Oh. Right." Kate felt a little foolish, but she pushed it away. Melissa probably hadn't said that to make a point that Kate wasn't watching, but the comment stung just the same.

What's wrong with me? Kate wondered. Somehow she had to get past questioning everything Melissa said or did, but it was hard to do after months of Melissa looking down on the three of them—not to mention dissing the Ferrises' barn when she first brought her horse there.

Kate turned her attention to the field stretched out alongside the road. No horses. Figured. "Hey, Tori?"

"Huh?"

Kate dropped her voice. "Do you think Melissa still hates us?"

"She doesn't act like she does." Tori kept her voice barely above a whisper. "You're worrying again, aren't you?"

"I suppose. I'll try to quit."

"Good. Let's have fun today and see if we can find that mystery horse."

"Mystery Rider, you mean."

"It's a mystery horse, too. It's not like we know anything about it." Tori pedaled a little harder as they started up a slight rise. "Except he's the most beautiful horse I've ever seen. You know, I've never cared that much about horses until now. I mean, I like them okay, but that one is … somehow special."

Melissa rode up close behind them. "What breed do you think he is?"

Kate shivered, thankful she'd heard the crunch of Melissa's tires. There was no way Melissa could have overheard what they'd said a few seconds earlier, but it still worried Kate. She needed to be more careful. "I couldn't really tell, but I'd guess it's an Arabian. He wasn't tall and streamlined like a Thoroughbred, and his head is more refined than a Quarter horse, but that's all I could see."

"So probably not a jumper," Melissa reasoned. "I doubt he's being stabled at any of the barns in the area that take boarders, but you never know. Maybe we should check a couple of them in case?"

"Good idea!" Kate tried to force some enthusiasm, but she wanted to smack her forehead instead. Why couldn't she come up with some of the things Melissa kept suggesting? It was like the girl was out to show her up, one way or another. If only she could tell if Melissa was acting or being genuine ... but all Kate could do was pray her rival—or was it her *former* rival?—wasn't out to pull a prank that would hurt them all.

Kate and her three friends, shoulders slumped in disappointment, left the boarding stable where three of them had worked for a few weeks in the spring. No one had seen a black horse of any kind, much less one being ridden at night.

Tori swung her leg over her bike. "So what next?"

Melissa crossed her arms over her chest and fixed her gaze on Kate. "Are you sure you saw this horse and rider? You didn't dream it?"

Kate bristled and barely kept from glaring at Melissa. "Of course not. We all saw it, not just me."

Melissa tossed her long blonde curls and smirked. "Fine, but you've got to admit it's strange that no one else we've talked to has seen them. Especially with them riding down a public road. Any number of people should have driven by."

"Yeah, but how many of those people have we talked to?" Colt countered, his smile lopsided. "It's not like horses aren't common around here. Most people driving past in the evening probably wouldn't even have noticed. Just because no one we've talked to has seen them doesn't mean they don't exist."

Kate blew out a breath, thankful for Colt's sensible reply and calm attitude. She'd been ready to flare up and ask Melissa if she was accusing them of lying, but she was so glad she hadn't. Arguing or getting angry wasn't going to help them find the Mystery Rider and horse. "Right, Colt. So what do you suggest? Start knocking on doors?"

"Nope." He straddled his bike and perched on the seat, one foot balancing him. "We wait."

Tori arched a brow. "For them to ride by again? What good will that do? We've tried to get the woman to talk to us twice, and she's not interested. She takes off and doesn't look back."

"I know. But how fast can she go when it's almost dark? I say we have our bikes ready and follow next time. See where she goes."

"Then what?" Melissa hadn't relaxed her tense stance.

Kate glanced at her. What was with Melissa today, anyway? It was as if she was angry all the time, or suspicious or something. Kate was really beginning to regret inviting the girl into their circle.

Colt smiled. "We'll worry about that when the time comes. Since it's not safe to be riding bikes in the pitch-dark, we'll probably only be able to follow for a short while, so we can get home while it's still light. If we're lucky, we'll see where she goes. Then we can talk about checking it out the next day. Or not." He looked at each of the girls in turn. "So who's in?"

"Me." Kate spoke quickly, hoping Tori would say yes while secretly wishing Melissa would say no and head home.

Kate's heart sank when Tori and Melissa both nodded and agreed at the same time. They were going to be stuck with Melissa and her attitude for at least another day.

Kate was thankful her parents didn't mind her riding her bike with friends in the evening. At least it wouldn't be dark for another hour, and dusk wouldn't come for another twenty minutes or so. The four of them sat on her back porch watching the road, bikes parked nearby.

Melissa rested her elbows on her knees. "What if she doesn't come tonight? We waited last night and nothing. This might be a waste of time. I still haven't seen this Mystery Rider of yours."

Her attitude's really getting old, Kate thought. "It's not like we have a lot of choice, unless we want to forget it," she said aloud.

"We haven't done any more planning for the parade lately," Melissa replied. "Maybe we should go inside and do that instead."

Tori's face fell. "If it's okay with everyone, I'd like to wait a little longer. It's almost the time she came by a few days ago."

Colt held up his hand. "Shh. No more talking. I thought I heard something."

Kate strained to listen but only heard crickets chirping and frogs peeping. "Nothing."

"Wait." Colt narrowed his eyes. "There it is again."

A dawning realization lit the other girls' faces, and Kate sucked in a shallow breath. She heard it too. Hoofbeats on the gravel not far up the road. She sprang to her feet. "Let's get on our bikes and be ready," she whispered.

Colt shook his head. "Not yet. We don't want her to notice us sitting here. Let's hold still until she goes past."

Kate waited, gazing up the road where the Mystery Rider had appeared last time. "Yes!" She pumped her fist in the air. "There she is, cloaked, hooded, and trotting." She eyed Colt. "How long should we wait before we follow?"

"Let her get past the house and have her back to us. Then I say we wait at least another minute so she doesn't notice us."

Melissa scowled. "But what if she goes around the corner and disappears? We don't want to lose her."

Kate bit her lip to keep from laughing. Melissa finally believed them and was now more worried and excited than they were. "There aren't any side roads up ahead," Kate quietly explained, "so I think we're safe. I agree with Colt. We don't want her to notice four kids on bikes following her."

"Right." Tori gave a quick nod, her focus fixed on the rider going past. "She has that hood pulled up so far that I still can't see her face. What's with that anyway? It's too warm for any kind of jacket, much less a hood."

They huddled together until the horse was out of sight, then climbed on their bikes and pushed off. Kate's heart thudded so hard she could feel it. If only they didn't lose sight of the woman and could solve the mystery …

The four friends pedaled across the lawn and onto the road. Colt led the group, but he didn't ride as fast as Kate would have liked. "Hey, Colt. Let's go faster or we'll lose her," she urged.

He glanced back over his shoulder. "We don't want to catch up with her either, but I guess we can go a little faster." He increased his speed, and the girls followed.

An owl hooted in the branches of a tree they passed, and Kate shivered. She wasn't superstitious at all, but that sound was creepy. She could see up the road a ways, but there was no sign of the horse and rider. Her mind raced back to the question Melissa had asked. What would they do if they found out where the woman lived? Why was she being so secretive, only riding the horse in the late evening and keeping her face hidden? None of it made sense.

They approached a corner, and Colt called back, "We should see them up ahead, and we might need to slow down so we don't spook them."

Kate tensed as the corner approached. After the long, sweeping curve, it took a couple of minutes to hit the straightaway on the far side. The light from the moon had increased, and the trees cast long, spiky shadows. Kate could still see the road all the way to the next corner, some distance ahead.

Not a thing moved along the entire stretch. The horse and rider had disappeared like a wisp of smoke on the wind.

Chapter Four

All four bikes skidded to a stop at nearly the same time, spraying gravel from beneath their tires.

Kate balanced one foot on the ground and stared ahead, then peered over her shoulder the way they'd come. "What's going on? Where'd they go?"

Colt pushed his bike toward them from his position in the lead, shaking his head. "Weird."

Tori shivered. "No, it's not weird; it's spooky. I say we go home."

Melissa laughed. "You're a bunch of babies if you give up right when it's getting interesting."

Melissa's mocking words made Kate mad. She sucked in a long breath and let it out slowly before replying. "I don't think Tori is being a baby at all, and Colt is right. It is weird. The horse and rider were ahead of us. We all saw them." She narrowed her eyes. "Do *you* know where they went?"

Melissa gripped the handlebars so tight, her knuckles whitened. "Why should I? Are you accusing me of something, Kate?" She pushed her bike a couple of inches toward Kate. "You've had it in for me since the day I came to help you paint the fence. If you don't want me here, say so. I'll go home, and I won't bug you again."

Kate stared at Melissa, hardly able to believe what she'd heard. *She* had it in for Melissa? It had been the other way around from the time they'd met. Anger brimmed. More than anything right now, Kate wanted to throw Melissa's words back at her and say exactly what she thought.

But at that instant, her mother's comment returned: *So it's okay to get even with someone if she wasn't kind to you in the past?*

Kate's tense muscles relaxed. "I don't want you to go home, Melissa, and I'm sorry if I made you feel that way. I thought you were only hanging around us because you're bored." She didn't want to admit how much she'd distrusted Melissa's motives. "I mean, it's not like we were ever friends before I let you use Capri in the horse show. You don't owe me anything. I did it because I wanted to."

"Right. And not because you felt sorry for me because of my mother." Melissa almost growled the words.

Colt pushed in closer, his bike tire bumping into Melissa's and sidetracking her attention. "So what if we did? What's wrong with caring about how someone feels, especially if she's hurting?"

Melissa's eyes widened. "I don't want your pity."

Tori gave a slow nod. "Yeah, I get that. I thought Kate was only being nice to me at first because I'm different."

Melissa scowled. "What's that supposed to mean?"

"You know, I'm not white like you guys. I don't fit in all the time. Kids think I'm a foreigner because my dad is from Mexico, even though I was born here." Tori shrugged. "Sometimes that hurts, and when anyone goes out of their way to be nice to me, I don't always trust them. Until they prove they really want to know me and be friends." She lifted her head and smiled. "Like Kate did for you and me."

Melissa's grip on her handlebars loosened, and her body sagged. "Right. I didn't know you felt that way, Tori." She raised her chin, and tears glistened in her eyes. "Did I make you feel bad because you're different?"

Tori hesitated. "Yeah. Kind of. Sometimes. But you weren't mean like some of the kids. You mostly just ignored me."

A tear trickled down Melissa's cheek. "I'm sorry. I didn't realize …"

Warmth rushed over Kate. She set her bike down and reached to touch Melissa's arm. She suddenly got it. All this time, Melissa had been hurting, thinking they'd only been feeling sorry for her and not wanting to be friends. "Hey. What happened to your other friends? Why aren't you hanging out with them? Not that we don't want you, but I'm curious."

Melissa swiped the back of her hand across her eyes. "They dumped me when they found out we aren't rich. Mom kept it hidden for a long time, but now the bill collectors are coming, and I don't have money to throw around anymore. I guess most of my friends didn't like me for myself, huh?" Her smile wavered. "But seriously, I don't want to barge in on you guys."

Kate exchanged glances with Tori and Colt, then told Melissa, "Silly. You aren't barging in. We made you the head of our parade committee, remember? We wouldn't have done that if we didn't want you around. Right, guys?"

Tori and Colt grinned, and Colt patted Melissa on the shoulder. "Now that all the girlie, emotional stuff is settled, how about we decide what we're going to do about this mystery horse?"

Late the next morning, Tori, Colt, and Melissa sat around the table on the Ferrises' outdoor patio. Kate set down a tray of pink lemonade and four glasses filled with ice, then slipped into the empty seat by Tori. "Help yourselves."

Colt removed the piece of straw from between his teeth and tossed it on the grass, then reached for the pitcher. "Thanks. So what do we do now?"

"I've been doing some checking on the parade rules," Melissa reported. "Want to hear them?"

"Yeah!" the other three chorused at once.

Melissa sobered. "It's going to cost all of us. There's an entry fee."

Tori groaned. "I didn't think of that. Great. How much?"

"A whopping two dollars and fifty cents each! Think we can handle it?" Melissa laughed.

Tori gaped at her, then chuckled. "You had me worried for a minute. I thought we'd have to do some kind of fund-raiser or something. Whew! That's great!"

"Yeah." Kate nodded. "Is that it?"

"We have to fill out a form and tell them if we're entering as individuals or a group, but since we're representing the barn and it would only be ten dollars for the whole group, I figured that's the way to go, right?" Melissa cocked her head.

"For sure," Colt said. "What else?"

"We give them a description of our entry for the parade announcer, show up at the starting point ahead of time, and stay in line during the parade. It says we can throw candy along the sidewalk in front of the crowd if we want to, or just wave and smile, and that's it. Sounds simple enough."

Kate leaned back in her chair. "Awesome. I figured we'd have to have a designated pooper-scooper to go behind the horses."

"I read somewhere that some towns make horses wear diapers," Tori added. "Can you imagine? That makes a pooper-scooper sound pretty good."

Colt hooted with laughter. "No way. You're making that up."

"Am not. Mom found it on the Internet and told me about it when I said we wanted to be in the parade. She was worried about having to make a diaper big enough to fit Mr. Gray, Kate." Her eyes twinkled.

Kate gagged. "Nasty. Hopefully they won't change the rules for this parade."

Melissa giggled. "Any of our horses would probably turn into bucking broncos if you tried to strap a diaper under their tails. I'd sure like to see a picture of someone who actually did it!"

Colt sobered. "So, that's all we need to do? Come up with ten bucks, fill out the application, and show up on time?"

Melissa nodded. "But remember, we still need some kind of banner with the barn name on it. Either draped behind the saddle with the words on both sides or on a pole that we carry like a flag."

Tori winced. "I think I need both hands on the reins. It's going to be scary enough riding Mr. Gray in a parade without trying to hang on to a flagpole. No thanks."

"I agree," Colt announced. "I've ridden in one parade, and my horse did great, but not every horse does. We don't want any accidents."

Tori paled. "Maybe I should stay home. Or I can be the pooper-scooper if they say we need one."

Kate took a sip of her lemonade, then set down the glass. "No way. Mr. Gray is an old hand. The previous owner said he'd been ridden in several parades."

"O-kay ..." Tori didn't look convinced. "But I'll still volunteer for cleanup duty if we need it."

Melissa hugged her. "You'll do fine, Tori. We should get back to planning the banner, right? Any ideas?"

They spent another thirty minutes tossing around ideas for material and lettering. Finally Colt heaved to his feet. "Sorry, girls, but this is definitely not guy stuff. I think I'll go hang out with Pete and read to him or something."

Kate grinned. "You mean you aren't an accomplished seamstress? Sheesh. And here I thought you'd be doing all the work once we figured out the details." She plopped her elbows on the glass tabletop. "I think we've brainstormed enough. You got any ideas for what we should do now about the Mystery Rider and her horse?"

Colt thudded back in his seat. "Whew. Glad that's over and we can move on. Not that I don't want to ride in the parade, but girl's stuff is, well, girl's stuff, if you know what I'm sayin'."

Tori poked her elbow into his side. "And you're out-numbered, so you might want to be careful what you say."

He groaned. "Yes, boss."

She glanced around the small circle. "Anybody got any ideas?"

"I was thinking we need to go up the road and look for horseshoe prints leaving the road and going into the woods," Kate suggested. "They couldn't have vanished during the night. It's not like they're ghosts or anything."

Tori shivered. "I sure hope not."

Melissa laughed, but her tone was kind instead of her usual mocking laugh. "If it is a ghost, we'll protect you, Tori." She sobered and faced Kate. "I think that's a really good idea. I'm not sure the horse is shod, but if it went off the road and onto any dirt, we might be able to find tracks. When do you guys want to try?"

Colt and Kate both jumped to their feet. "Right now," they echoed.

Kate motioned toward the house. "I'll check with Mom and make sure it's okay. Since it's daylight and not far away, I don't think she'll mind."

She rushed into the house, excitement battling with nervous apprehension in her heart. They still hadn't settled the question of what they'd do if they ever found the horse and rider.

Chapter Five

Kate and her friends parked their bikes against two trees right around the corner where they'd last glimpsed the Mystery Rider in the distance. "Are you sure this is a good idea, leaving our bikes here?" Kate asked no one in particular.

"Yep," Colt said casually. "No one is going to steal four bikes at once, and they'll be in sight all the way up the road. If we find where the horse turned off, we can come back and get them. But it's going to be hard to see any prints if we're riding. We need to walk and keep our eyes on the ground."

"Okay, I guess that's smart." Kate edged to the side of the road. "So do we split up? Two of us on each side?"

Melissa crinkled her nose. "I didn't think about that. I'm not sure why I assumed they'd turn off this direction, but you're right, Kate. They could as easily have crossed the road and disappeared on the other side."

"Right." Colt beckoned to Tori. "You want to come with me, and Kate and Melissa can check this edge?"

Kate threw him a questioning look. He knew Tori and she were best friends, and that until last night, she'd been struggling with trusting Melissa. Was this some kind of test, or didn't he want to walk with Melissa? Either way, she couldn't very well say no. They'd already made Melissa feel like she wasn't wanted recently, and Kate couldn't do that again. "Sure. Come on, Melissa. You might be right, and we'll be the ones to find where they left the road."

Melissa grinned at Tori. "Or sprouted wings and flew over the treetops."

Tori smacked Melissa's arm. "We didn't see any wings on that horse, so I don't think that's gonna happen."

Melissa smirked. "I was thinking of something a little spookier."

"Like I'll be scared. Dead people don't come back to life anyway." Tori exhaled dramatically. "Come on, Colt. Let's go check out the other side of the road and see if we can solve this mystery."

"What's with her?" Melissa retorted. "I was only joking. Besides, my mom said reincarnation might be true. She's been checking out different religions lately and telling me some of what she's learned."

Kate's stomach lurched. She hadn't expected that they would talk about stuff like that. What should she say—that Melissa's mom didn't know what she was talking about and was listening to people who didn't know God? That might offend Melissa. But Kate couldn't lie and pretend she didn't care or didn't have an opinion, when she agreed with Tori.

As they started along the edge of the road, Kate was thankful they needed to keep their eyes on the ground. "She was only telling you what she believes."

"Yeah, well, how is it any better than what anyone else believes?" Melissa stuffed her hands in her jeans pockets and scanned the hard-packed dirt.

"She and I, and Colt too, believe that the Bible tells us what's true. It says that once a person dies, they don't come back. They either go to heaven or hell. Except Jesus did, and there have been people raised from the dead, but I mean it's not normal."

"So what … you guys are religious nuts? I always knew there was something different about you." Melissa's tone had drifted back to its old snideness, but somehow Kate sensed curiosity as well.

"No, we're Christians, that's all."

"So, religious nuts. Kooks," Melissa said in a sly voice, as if testing to see if Kate still wanted her around.

Suddenly Kate got it. All this time, she'd been thinking about herself and her friends, worried that Melissa was out to get them, when God had sent Melissa to them so they could tell her about Him. Wow. That was cool! Kate couldn't help it. She laughed.

Melissa jerked to a stop and glared. "So now you're laughing at me? Maybe I'll head home."

Kate tried to control her giggling. "No. I'm sorry. I wasn't laughing at you. I admit, it does seem funny that you'd want to hang out with kids you think are kooks, but that's not it. I was laughing at myself for being so stupid."

Melissa swung around, her mouth pressed in a firm line. "Explain."

"All this time I've been thinking you hated us and you were mean. Well, maybe you did hate us a little at first, but I don't think you've ever intentionally been mean."

Melissa crossed her arms over her chest. "What exactly are you saying?"

Kate kicked at a pinecone. "You said your mom is searching and checking out different religions. I'm wondering if maybe you're searching for what makes the three of us happy. You said you noticed we're different. We didn't cut you off when we found out you don't have money, 'cause it doesn't matter to us. We like people for who they are and how they act, not for the stuff they have." She hunched a shoulder. "And I guess part of that is how we've been raised. But all three of us know Jesus personally—like, He's our friend—so I think it goes past how we were raised, if that makes any sense."

Melissa dropped her arms to her sides. "Not even a tiny bit. I figured you'd start yelling at me when I said you were kooks. That you'd tell me to get lost and that you don't want me to hang around anymore. I don't get you, Kate Ferris. Not at all."

Kate looped her hand around Melissa's arm. "Maybe you will if you hang around long enough. Now let's see if we can find those hoofprints. Colt and Tori are way ahead of us, and they haven't found a thing yet, so I think we're going to get lucky soon!"

Melissa at first froze at Kate's touch but then smiled. "Sounds good to me. Let's go."

They scanned the roadside for several yards with no results. The brush and trees grew thicker in this section, making it harder to see the ground. Kate and Melissa had covered another short section when Melissa stopped abruptly and grabbed Kate's hand. "Look." She pointed toward the dense brush.

Kate stared but didn't see anything unusual. "What? There's nothing there."

Melissa released her hold on Kate and gestured. "You're not looking high enough. See that low-hanging branch beyond the brush?"

Kate concentrated. "Yeah. And?"

"There's a small piece of black fabric caught on the end."

"Wow! You've got great eyes to spot that."

Melissa ducked her head. "My dad always used to say I could find anything that was lost. We'd better holler at Tori and Colt so they don't get too far ahead."

"Right. I'll get them. You keep your eyes on that branch." Kate jogged up the road until she wasn't far from her two friends. "Hey, guys. We think Melissa found something. Unless you've found tracks, you might want to come check this out."

Colt and Tori ran across the gravel road, and Colt reached Kate first. "What's up? You find hoofprints?"

"No." Kate pointed. "Maybe something better. The brush was too close to the road, so we didn't see any tracks. Come on, I'll show you."

They raced one another back to the spot where Melissa waited, then stopped. Tori shaded her eyes against the summer sun peeking through the branches. "What are we looking for?"

Melissa explained and started to walk toward the branch, but Colt held up a hand. "Wait. Let's make sure there's no poison oak or bramble bushes before we plow through this thicket. Better yet, is there an easier way around to where that branch is hanging?" He searched the ground around the clump of brush and grunted. "This way. There's a narrow path past this tangle of weeds. It goes around the big, thick stuff and comes out on the other side, not far from that tree." He led the way, and the girls followed; then they halted under the tree.

Tori squinted at the branch hanging about four or five feet above their heads. "So you think the Mystery Rider went under here and snagged her hood?"

Kate smiled at Melissa. "Yep. And we wouldn't have found it if it hadn't been for Melissa."

Colt extended his fist and gave Melissa a fist bump. "Way to go. Now what?"

Kate froze. She'd been so excited about their find, she hadn't thought any further. "I'm not sure. Maybe see if we can find tracks and follow them?"

Tori glanced into the woods that darkened as they grew denser. "Um … really?"

Melissa touched Tori's shoulder. "Yeah. But it's okay if you don't want to, Tori. We'll understand."

Tori's eyes widened. "Thanks, but if you guys are going, I am too. We're in this together, right?"

Kate grinned. "Right. You're my best friend, and I'm not leaving you behind. I think Melissa's right. I say we follow the path, if there is one, and see where it leads. We'll all watch each other's backs. Agreed, Colt?"

He stared up at the branch with the piece of cloth caught on the tip. "I'm in." He waggled his brows. "Let's go see what we can scare up. I'm ready for an adventure."

Chapter Six

Kate stayed right on Colt's heels as they pushed through the dense brush, and Tori and Melissa pressed close behind them. After what seemed like an hour but was probably only a few minutes, they got to the edge of the deep stand of trees and halted to catch their breath. Kate glanced at Tori. "You doing okay?"

"Yep. Great, now that we're not being scratched by branches anymore, and I can see the sun again." Her friend pulled a tangle of leaves out of her hair.

Melissa peered over Kate's shoulder. "Do you see anything?"

"Nothing. Just an open field." Disappointment hit Kate hard. They'd found a path of sorts most of the way and occasionally noted hoofprints, but those had ended when they hit that final patch of brush. There was no sign of tracks there either.

Colt squatted and peered at the ground, running his hand over the thick weeds. "It's possible the horse came this way, and the weeds and grass sprang back up, but I don't see any impressions. Why come this way, and why all the secrecy? I don't get it."

"Me neither. So what now?" Kate wasn't sure what to do anymore, and she hoped one of the others would have a good idea.

Silence was her only answer for several long seconds. Then Tori held up her hand. Kate knew what she'd say—go home and give this up.

Tori put her hand down and gave a sheepish grin. "Sorry. I kind of felt like I was in school. Anyway, we've come this far. I think we should walk across the field and see if there's anything there. If there isn't, we go home. I mean, what could it hurt, right?"

Melissa's eyes rounded. "Seriously? Wow. I'm impressed, Tori. I was going to suggest we give up, but if you're willing, I am. How about you guys?" She looked from Kate to Colt.

Colt nodded. "Sure. Let's do it."

Kate smiled. "I'm in. Tori's right, we've come this far. And if we go home now, we'll probably always wonder if we missed something by not going a little farther."

They stepped out of the woods and headed across the open meadow. Kate looked around her, loving the sense of peace in the quiet spot. Grass and purple wildflowers dotted the field, and a robin fluttered from an ancient apple tree. "I wonder if this used to be an old homestead. Look—is that a stone fence that fell down?"

Colt stopped a few yards from where Kate pointed. "I think it's the remains of a stone foundation from a small house or a cabin." He shielded his eyes against the bright sun. "There's a fence ahead made of wood rails. Looks like some of it's starting to fall down. Should we check it out?"

The girls nodded, and the four spread out in a line as they walked the direction he indicated. Minutes passed, and they slowed as they neared the fence. Tori put her finger to her lips. "Shh. There's a house over there." She waved off to her left. "And look! I see the black horse!" Her voice rose in excitement.

"Awesome!" Kate breathed the word. She leaned her arms on the rail fence. "Now what?"

Colt glanced from one to the other. "I say we get a little closer. Maybe we'll see the woman outside, and we can tell her we like her horse. If she's friendly, we can ask questions and maybe find out what she's up to."

No one spoke for a minute. Then Tori frowned. "Uh, I'm not so sure that's a good idea. Wouldn't that be trespassing?"

Melissa scanned the fence in both directions. "There aren't any signs posted. We're just going for a friendly visit. I can't see that she'll be upset over some kids asking about her horse."

Kate hated to go against Tori, but she was dying to know more about this horse and the Mystery Rider. "I guess she can only tell us to get lost. Tori, will you be mad if I say we should go?"

She hunched a shoulder. "Naw. It's okay. I'd like to get a closer look at that horse, but I don't want to get in trouble either. If you guys say we should do this, then I will too."

Colt gave a short nod. "Good. I'll lead, and we'll take it slow."

He stepped on the bottom rail, then vaulted over the top bar. He turned and waited for the girls to climb over or through the rails. "Let's not talk, all right? We don't want to spook that woman if she's around."

They headed toward the two-story house with faded-green paint. The horse stood in a fenced pasture nearby, and as they got closer, he raised his head and whinnied. All of a sudden, the back door of the house burst open, and a small woman stepped onto the porch, her long gray hair sticking out in all directions. She stood under the porch roof, and the shadow fell across her face, but a ray of sun glinted off the barrel of the rifle she clutched. She peered around, apparently trying to see what had alerted the horse.

Kate, Colt, Tori, and Melissa halted where they stood, about a hundred feet away. Kate's hands started to shake. "What should we do?"

Before anyone could answer, the old woman raised the rifle and waved it in the air. "I told you kids not to bother me anymore! Get off my property!"

Melissa, Kate, and Colt turned and raced for the fence. It wasn't until they'd run several strides that Kate looked for Tori. Her friend stood frozen where they'd left her, and Kate skidded to a halt. "Tori! Come on! Don't stand there and get shot!"

Tori seemed to wake up, then shook her head. She raised her hand toward the woman, whose face was still in the shadows. "We don't mean any harm. We only wanted to tell you we love your horse. We're so sorry we bothered you." She pivoted, then walked toward Kate but kept peeking over her shoulder.

Kate held her breath as Tori moved; then she glanced at the old woman and gasped. She had placed the rifle down on the porch floor and had sunk into a chair, her hands covering her face as though she was crying.

Panting and shaking, Kate and her friends burst out of the brush at the road where they'd stashed their bikes, but Tori was strangely quiet. Kate grabbed her friend's hand and tugged her the last several feet. "What was all that about? Why did you talk to that woman when she had a gun pointed at us?"

Tori shook her head. "She wasn't going to hurt us."

Melissa crossed her arms over her chest and scowled. "And how do you know that?"

Colt nodded. "Yeah, Tori. You could have been hurt. I didn't even realize you weren't with us until I heard you say something, but I was too far away to understand what was happening."

Tori looked from one to the other, her face calm. "She loves that horse."

Melissa rolled her eyes. "What does that have to do with anything?"

"Didn't you notice? Her house is in terrible shape, the porch roof was practically falling down, she's dressed in old clothes, and her hair was a mess, but that horse was perfect. His mane and coat are so silky and shiny, it looks like he's been brushed for hours every day. The fence around his paddock is practically new, and he has fresh hay and a shiny water trough. He's not neglected, and he didn't act scared, just curious. No one takes that good care of an animal unless they love them, or they're worth a lot of money. Since she doesn't look like she has much money, I doubt he's supervaluable—except to her."

"Yeah … so?" Melissa continued to stare, but she uncrossed her arms.

"So I don't think she's as mean as she tried to act. I think maybe some other kids have been harassing her, and she thought we were them. She was protecting her property, like anyone would do."

Kate bit her lip. "I don't think everyone would protect it with a rifle."

Tori planted her hands on her hips. "I agree, but she's an old lady, and if she lives alone and people have been bugging her, she might feel she has to do that."

Kate thought for a moment, remembering what she'd seen at the very end before she ran. "Did you notice she put the rifle down before we took off?"

Tori gave a sad smile. "Yeah. And I think she was crying."

Colt's eyes widened. "Huh?"

A car drove past, kicking up dust. Kate waved toward their bikes. "We'd better head home. But Tori's right. I saw the lady cover her face with her hands, and her shoulders were shaking."

"Weird," Melissa said. "What's up with that?"

All of them grabbed their bikes and climbed on, then headed back toward Kate's house. No one spoke as they pedaled their way home, but Kate kept an eye on Tori, worried about what might be going on in her friend's head. Something didn't feel right about how Tori was acting, but Kate couldn't quite figure it out. She needed to get her alone and see if she'd tell her. Maybe

Tori didn't want to say any more in front of Melissa, or even Colt, but she and Kate were best friends. Kate knew in her heart that Tori would tell her everything as soon as they were alone.

Chapter Seven

Kate and Tori sat on Kate's bed after telling Melissa and Colt good-bye. Tori had barely spoken after they'd returned and parked their bikes in Kate's backyard. Since no one seemed to have any interest in planning their parade costumes or talking about anything else, their other friends left. They agreed to get together again sometime the next day, but Kate had whispered to Tori, asking her to stay a little longer.

Kate scooted up against the headboard and tucked a pillow behind her back, while Tori sat cross-legged at the end of the bed. "So what's up, Tori? Something's bugging you, and it's got to be that horse."

Tori ducked her head. "That woman looked so sad, Kate. I think there's something wrong. Maybe even something worse than kids bothering her."

Surprise surged through Kate. This wasn't what she'd expected. She knew Tori had fallen in love with the black horse, but she didn't realize she'd be worried about the woman. On the other hand, her friend was one of the kindest kids she'd ever met, and if anyone would feel sorry for someone who threatened to shoot them, it would be Tori. She frowned at Tori's bowed head. "I guess that's possible. But there's nothing we can do about it."

"Why not?" Tori lifted her head and met Kate's eyes.

"You didn't see that rifle and hear her tell us to leave? You really want to try that again?"

Tori's dark eyes blazed. "Yeah. I do. But just you and me, not Colt and Melissa. I think there were too many of us, and we scared her."

Kate stared at Tori. This couldn't be for real. "No way. That's nuts. I mean, next time she might shoot us!"

"Naw. I don't think so. If she was going to, then I think she would have shot in the air to really scare us. Besides, I told you she was crying. That doesn't sounds like someone crazy enough to shoot at a bunch of kids."

"Maybe, but I'm not willing to take that chance." Kate figured that would end the discussion. She'd always been the bold one, and Tori was always so tenderhearted.

"Fine." Tori worried her bottom lip with her teeth.

Kate breathed a sigh of relief and settled deeper into the pillow. Maybe she should go get them a soda or something or suggest they call Colt and Melissa to come back and do more planning, now that this subject was settled.

Tori leaned forward, bracing her elbows on her crossed legs. "If you don't want to come, then I'll go alone."

Kate almost fell off the bed in shock. She'd never seen Tori act like this before, and she couldn't believe how firm her friend's voice was, or how determined her face appeared. "Seriously? You want to go back there, and you'd go alone if I don't come? Why?"

"I'm not sure." Tori tapped her chest. "But I feel it in here. Like God is telling me it's the right thing to do. That we're supposed to help her somehow. I don't know any more than that. But I won't be mad if you don't want to come. I understand."

Kate sat up straight. "No way will I let you go alone." She shuddered. "That old woman could shoot you and bury you behind the house, and no one would ever know. You're my best friend, and if I can't talk you out of it, then I'm going with you."

A smile lit Tori's face, and her eyes sparkled. "You'd do that for me?"

Kate didn't hesitate. "You bet. You've always backed me up, and I'll do the same for you. That's what friends are for, right?"

Tori beamed. "Right. I've never had that kind of a friend before you came along, that's all."

"So what's your plan?"

Tori's smile faded. "I'm not sure. I hadn't thought that far."

"And what do we tell Colt and Melissa?"

Tori shook her head. "Nothing. I don't want anyone else involved. We have to do this alone, Kate."

"O-kay …" Kate didn't like it, but Tori was the boss on this one. If she didn't go along with her friend, Tori might decide to do it alone, and that wasn't an option. "But we need some kind of plan. We can't just walk up to the house again. She'll chase us off like last time."

"I agree." They were quiet for a minute before Tori spoke again. "We could bake cookies or brownies or something and take them to her as an apology for upsetting her today."

Kate nodded. "I suppose. I'm not crazy about cutting through the woods again, though. I sure wish we knew if there was another way in."

"I saw a driveway on the far side of the paddock where the horse was."

"Seriously? Man, I didn't notice anything other than that rifle." Kate stared at her friend in awe.

"I don't know where it comes out, so I suppose we'll have to go in the same way." Tori's shoulders drooped. "I wish we'd stayed longer and tried to talk to her."

Kate raised her brows. "Uh … she told us to leave. I don't think that was a good time to try to talk."

"I know. So, what do you think about taking cookies?"

"Sure. Mom won't care if we bake a batch. Are we going to tell our parents?"

Tori worried her lip again. "Could we tell them we're taking cookies to an old lady who's lonely, and not tell them the rest?"

Kate hesitated. They wouldn't be telling a lie, but they wouldn't be telling the entire truth either. "I'm not sure. I guess we can try that, but if my mom or your mom asks any questions, we'll have to tell them more. Do you care if we tell them we're taking the cookies to the Mystery Rider, but we don't know her name?"

Tori smiled. "That's a great idea. We'll tell them we found her house and want to do something nice for her. I don't think they'll object to that."

Kate nodded, but it still didn't feel right. She wasn't sure Mom and Dad would approve if they knew everything, but she couldn't take the chance that Tori would go alone and get herself into trouble. "All right. When do you want to go?"

"Colt said something about working on the parade stuff sometime tomorrow. How about we bake a big batch of cookies to share with Colt and Melissa so they won't ask questions. Then after they leave, we'll head over on our own. We'll ask them to come in the morning so we'll have the afternoon free. Sound good?"

"Yeah, I guess." Kate shoved her doubts to the side. She wished they could at least tell Colt. He was sensible and didn't rush into stuff the way she sometimes did—but she'd promised not to tell, and she wouldn't break her word. She felt stuck between two bad choices, but her friendship with Tori was important, and she couldn't let her down. All she could do was pray she wasn't making a bad decision and they didn't find themselves in more trouble than they could handle.

The next morning, Kate swung open her front door a few seconds after the doorbell chimed.

"Hey, guys. I'm glad you made it. Tori's already here."

Melissa stepped inside, with Colt right on her heels, and his nose went up in the air. He sniffed. "Wow. Something smells awesome."

Kate grinned. "We've been baking. We thought we might need a little brain food to help us while we're planning." A twinge of guilt hit her. If only she could tell Colt and Melissa about their plans, she wouldn't feel so alone, but a promise was a promise.

"What kind of cookies are they?" Colt kept sniffing as he headed toward the kitchen.

Kate giggled. "You look like a bloodhound on a trail. Chocolate chip oatmeal with coconut and walnuts. The coconut keeps them soft, and we put tons of chocolate chips in them. Dad likes them better with raisins, so we're making a panful that way too. But Tori and I voted for chocolate in the rest of them."

Colt closed his eyes. "Mmm-mmm. I think I'm going to eat until I get sick."

Melissa rolled her eyes. "Boys can be so dramatic."

Colt's eyes snapped open. "Now that's funny. I'm a growing boy, and I love cookies. There's nothing dramatic about it. *Girls* are the dramatic ones."

Kate grabbed them both and pulled them the rest of the way to the kitchen. "Quit arguing and get some cookies and a glass of milk. We'll sit at the table to talk."

Melissa huffed but didn't argue.

Colt grinned. "I'll stop arguing if I have my mouth full of cookies. Besides, I got the last word, so I win." He dodged sideways as Melissa's elbow shot toward his ribs. "Ha! Missed."

Kate's mom breezed into the kitchen, and Pete followed slowly behind. "Hi, kids. Mind if Pete and I have a few cookies? His tutor is here, and I'm sure she'd appreciate a couple too."

"Sure, Mom. Hey, Pete. Are you having a good time with Mrs. Ingersoll?"

Pete kept his gaze on the plate of cookies. "Cookies."

Melissa stooped to Pete's level and held out the plate. "Here you go, bud." Her tone was soft, and the same one that Pete had often responded to.

He averted his gaze but reached out and took one, then slowly lifted it to his mouth.

Kate touched his hair, but he shrank back. "Pete, can you tell Melissa thank you?" She wished this was one of his good days when he'd let her touch him, but sometimes he became more withdrawn when his special teacher came, while on other days he seemed to blossom.

He took a bite of cookie. "No."

When he was in a mood like this, there was no point in pushing. Kate glanced at her mother, who smiled. "Come on, Pete. We'll take the cookies back to Mrs. Ingersoll, and you can have another one after you finish your work. Okay?" She extended her hand, but he ignored it and started humming a tune. Mom lowered her hand but stayed beside Pete. "Let's go, Son."

No one spoke as Kate's mom and Pete left the room, and in the quiet, Pete's humming could be heard all the way down the hall to her dad's study.

Melissa cleared her throat gently. "He's having a bad day, huh?"

Kate's eyes misted. "Sometimes I think he's improving so much. He talks more and occasionally looks someone in the eye—even lets us touch him or hug him. I start thinking maybe

the autistic thing is in the past. Then he goes backward like this."
Kate sighed. "I feel so bad for him."

Colt put his cookie on the plate in front of him. "But his good days are better than they were before, right? So he *is* improving."

Kate swallowed a lump in her throat. "I guess so … if I think of it that way. I just want him to be totally okay *now*, know what I mean?"

They all nodded.

Kate looked at her friends. "Thanks, guys. Now let's get to work and come up with super banners to drape over our horses."

Melissa held up her hand. "Before we do that, I found out some stuff about that old woman on the black horse."

Kate's heart pounded, and she chanced a glance at Tori, but her friend kept her eyes on Melissa. Kate leaned forward. "Did you talk to someone?"

"Yep. I called one of my mother's friends who knows everything about everybody, and she filled me in." Melissa dropped her voice and peered toward the kitchen door leading to the study. "I don't think your parents would want you going over there again, if they knew."

Colt drummed his fingers on the table. "Knew what? Spill it."

Melissa made a face at him, then turned to Kate and Tori. "Well, first of all, there's another way into her place. I don't know why she went down that trail, except maybe it's a shortcut. But if you keep on the road for another half mile or so, then turn right at the fork, her driveway is the first gravel road on the right. It's a short distance to her house from the road."

Kate groaned. "It would have been nice to find that before we went through all the brush. Plus, she might not have thought we were trying to do something bad if we'd come down her driveway instead of across her back pasture and over her fence."

"Did your mom's friend know anything else about her?" Colt asked.

"Yes. Some people say she's a witch and that's why she rides a black horse, but others say she's crazy. Someone disappeared from the area years ago, and rumor has it they might be buried behind her house. No one has ever proved it, but there's talk. My mom's friend says her house is haunted." Melissa waved her hand in the air. "Oh, and she has this long, jagged scar on her face, and I guess that's why she wears the hood." She shivered. "I wonder how that happened. Maybe she got in a knife fight with the person she buried on her property."

Colt laughed. "She's too little and too old to get in a fight with anyone. All that stuff you heard is gossip, and we shouldn't even listen to it. As for the scar and the hood, if that's true, she probably gets sick of people staring at her. I don't blame her." He reached for another cookie.

Melissa glared at him. "Some of it could be true. But no matter what, we solved the mystery, and we don't have to go back. I'm done with that place."

Tori nudged Kate's foot under the table, and Kate knew exactly what she was thinking. They'd made the right decision not to invite Melissa. But how about Colt? If the woman *was* dangerous, it would be awfully nice to have a boy around.

Chapter Eight

Kate shut the front door after Melissa and Colt left, then walked into the living room and slumped onto the couch. "Wow. Am I glad that's over. You don't know how many times I almost blurted out that we needed to hurry up and finish so you and I could get going." She grinned at Tori's horrified face. "Kidding. But I thought it plenty of times." She sat up. "You sure you want to go through with this? I told Mom we found out where our Mystery Rider lives, that she's an old lady who lives alone, and we're taking her cookies. That's all true, right?"

Tori gave a slow nod. "I told my mom the same thing. I don't believe all that stuff Melissa told us. She's not dangerous—she's lonely and scared. Do you think we're wrong not to tell our parents about her waving a rifle in the air? I'm afraid if we do, they won't let us go."

"We can tell them the whole story after we take the cookies, don't you think? We'll make friends and find out what's wrong with her. Then we can tell our parents, and they'll probably want to help her too. I bet they'll be proud of us when it's over."

Tori grinned. "Cool. I never thought of that. You ready to go?"

Kate pushed to her feet. "As soon as we put a bunch of cookies in a plastic bag. It's going to be hard to ride our bikes if we're carrying a plate."

"Right. Hey. Do you think we should write a note before we go, in case she's not there? We could leave it on her front porch with the cookies."

"Sure. But what are we gonna say?"

"Hmm … maybe *We're the kids who came to your house yesterday, and we're sorry we scared you.* Something like that. We can tell her we'd like to be friends, and we love her horse, and we brought her cookies. That way she won't worry about who came like she might if we just leave the bag there."

Kate headed for the kitchen. "That makes sense. Come on, your handwriting is better than mine. I'll get the cookies ready to go while you write the note."

A few minutes later, Kate stopped at the door of the study and waved at her mom. "We're taking the cookies now."

Mom looked up, her face distracted, and her gaze drifted from Kate to Pete, who sat with his head down, rocking and humming. Mrs. Ingersoll sat quietly beside him, waiting. Mom sighed and turned her attention back to Kate. "Don't be gone too long, honey. Remember, we don't know this lady. I'm sure she's fine—she can't be too much of a problem if she's as old as you say she is, but I still don't want you overstaying your welcome. Remember, hand her the cookies, then leave. You are not to go in her house. Agreed?"

"Yes, Mom. We won't, don't worry. And we'll hurry. I don't want to stay. Tori wants to ask about her horse, but that shouldn't take long." She lifted a hand and pivoted, then headed for the kitchen, where Tori waited. Kate hoped that everything she'd told her mom was true.

A couple of minutes later, Kate hung the bag of cookies over her bike handlebars. "Hey, I was thinking ..."

Tori narrowed her eyes. "You aren't wanting to back out, are you?"

"Nothing like that. I'm glad Melissa said she didn't want to go so we don't have to invite her, but how about Colt? I don't see any reason he can't come with us. Wouldn't it be safer to have him along if something goes wrong?"

Tori paused. "I'm not sure. What if he tries to talk us out of it?"

"You heard what he said. He didn't believe any of that stuff Melissa told us. He'll probably think it's a good idea to take the cookies and apologize for sneaking onto her property."

"Maybe, but why can't you and I go alone?"

Kate could tell Tori was wavering. She hated to pressure her friend, but she didn't want them to go alone, even if she didn't believe—or at least, she didn't *want* to believe—the stuff Melissa had said. "It's not that we *can't* go alone, but I think our parents would be happier if we didn't. You know, safety in numbers and all that. So, what do you think?"

Tori exhaled. "Okay. I guess it's smart, and I'll admit I'll feel better having him with us, as long as he doesn't tell us not to go. I'm going no matter what."

"Right. Want me to call him?"

"Sure. I'll wait here."

Kate returned to the backyard a short while later, her heart feeling much lighter. "He's going to meet us at the place where we left our bikes last time, where the path starts."

"Aren't we going up her driveway? I don't think we should try to sneak in the back way again." Tori swung her leg over her bike.

"We're not. Colt thought it was an easy place to meet, and we'll ride the rest of the way together."

"Sounds good. Let's go." Tori pushed off and headed toward the road.

Kate's stomach clenched at what might be coming. Tori was normally the timid one in their group, but her kindhearted nature had turned her into someone Kate barely recognized. All she could do was pray they weren't being foolish. She didn't believe in witches, but she didn't want anyone to get hurt if the woman was crazy.

Ten minutes later, Kate and Tori slowed to a stop on the edge of the road where Colt waited. He'd parked his bike against a tree and sat on top of a nearby stump, an ever-present blade of grass tucked in the side of his mouth. "Before we go any farther, you two have to tell me what you're up to. I agreed to come because I don't want you getting into trouble, but I'm not budging unless you convince me we're doing the right thing."

Tori slapped her palm on the handlebars of her bike. "I told you, Kate. We shouldn't have asked him. Let's go on our own, and he can go home."

Colt's eyes widened. "Whoa there, Tori. Sorry if I came across too strong, but you aren't dumping me that easy. You asked me to come, and I want to know what's up. All Kate told me was that you were taking cookies to the Mystery Rider. We forgot to ask Melissa if her mom's friend told her the woman's name."

"That's exactly what we're doing." Tori's chin tilted at a stubborn angle.

"But why are you going back after she waved that rifle and told us to get off her property? That doesn't make sense."

Kate held up her hand. "Tori thinks it's important we see her again. She—we—think the old lady is lonely and scared. She said something about kids coming back to bother her again, like she's been harassed and thought we were the same kids. We thought it would be nice to let her know it wasn't us, and that we're sorry for upsetting her." She smiled, hoping Colt would understand. "You thought the cookies were good, so we figured she might like them too."

Colt shifted the grass to the other side of his mouth. "I still don't know if it's a good idea, but it sounds like you're going no matter what I say."

Tori crossed her arms in determination. "Yep. We are."

"All right. Then I'll come, but you have to promise that we'll leave at the first sign of trouble. All the talk about her might be gossip, but it's possible she really *is* crazy or danger-ous. Agreed?"

Tori stared at him. "Agreed. But you can't go running off if she looks at us weird. I want a chance to give her the cookies. I even wrote a note in case she's not home."

"Sounds good. How come you didn't ask Melissa?"

"You'll have to ask Kate."

Kate straddled her bike. "She said she was done with that place. I didn't see any reason to ask her. Besides, we weren't even going to ask you until we heard what Melissa found out."

Colt blinked. "Why not? I didn't say I didn't want to go back."

"We figured too many people showing up might spook her again. Tori and I should go to the door alone, and you act as a lookout."

"Okay, but if anything goes wrong, you two get out of there fast. Got it?"

"Yes," both girls answered at the same time. A huge wave of relief swamped Kate. She'd had her doubts about the wisdom of her and Tori going alone, and Colt's presence made everything seem right.

They pedaled up the road for another half mile, keeping an eye out for the narrow gravel driveway Melissa had mentioned. Colt pointed to the right. "Looks like that might be it. You sure you want to go up there?"

Kate kept quiet, knowing what Tori would say, and she wasn't disappointed.

"Yes. Let's go." Tori pedaled faster and shot past Colt.

"Hey, wait up!" He stood on his pedals, increasing his speed, and pulled up behind her. "You aren't going in there alone. You've got to be smart, Tori. Wait for Kate and me."

She slowed to a stop, then put one foot on the gravel. "Sorry."

Kate and Colt stopped alongside Tori, and Kate took a second to catch her breath. "So, what's the plan? Do Tori and I ride up the driveway and you stay here, or what?"

Colt shook his head. "No way. I'm going with you at least until we can see the house. I won't go to the door, but I'm not letting you girls out of my sight."

"I think that's a good idea," Kate said.

They pushed their bikes around a curve and stopped to stare at the front of the small house they'd only seen from the rear on their last visit. The paint was peeling, and a few shingles had fallen off the roof, exposing the tar paper beneath. But most surprising was the white-washed picket fence surrounding the front yard brimming with flowers and neatly trimmed grass.

Tori gasped. "The backyard was dirt and bushes and an old porch that looked like it was about to fall over. I didn't expect something like this."

Colt balanced his bike and gripped the handlebars. "I'll wait here where I can see the front door. You guys knock, and if she doesn't come to the door right away, leave the bag and come right back. Okay?"

They nodded, laid their bikes on the ground, and headed for the gate in the fence. Tori pushed it open on silent hinges. Kate followed her through, and they both stood gazing around them.

Kate whistled. "I've never seen anything so pretty. Wow! Dahlias and daylilies and roses and tons of other stuff that I don't know the names of. Who'd have thought someone who's supposed to be crazy would do all this work?"

Tori gave a smug smile. "That's because she's not crazy; she's lonely. It doesn't mean she can't work in her yard or take care of her horse. People are so mean when they make up stories."

Kate's heart hammered as they almost tiptoed to the front porch. Would the old woman answer the door with the rifle in her arms? Would she yell at them and tell them to get off her property and act wild and crazy? Kate told herself to knock it off. That's what she got for believing Melissa's gossip.

Tori reached the door first and gave a tentative knock. They waited, but there was no sound of footsteps on the other side.

"Try it again, harder this time," Kate urged.

Tori knocked with more force, and they waited for what seemed like hours, but no one appeared. They turned to look at Colt.

He cupped his hands around his mouth, but the words drifted to them as a harsh whisper. "Leave the cookies and come on. She's not home."

Kate's knees were shaking as she placed the sack of cookies on a little bench by the door. Tori slipped the envelope containing their letter beneath it.

They turned to go but stopped short as a high-pitched wail, coming from the backyard, tore through the air.

Chapter Nine

Kate grabbed Tori's hand and dragged her from the porch and along the path to the gate, determined to get to their bikes and ride as hard as they could to her house. Colt straddled his bike and waved for them to hurry. They got to the gate, and Kate opened it and rushed through, not closing it behind her. She skidded to a stop by her bike and grabbed it from the ground, righting it and throwing her leg over the bar.

"Come on, Tori." Kate glanced over her shoulder. Where was she?

Colt let out an exasperated grunt. "Tori! What are you doing?"

Kate caught a glimpse of her friend slipping around the corner of the house toward the backyard. "No way! She can't go back there! That lady might really be crazy and hurt her." She dumped her bike on the ground at the same time Colt jumped off his, and they bolted in the direction Tori had taken.

Kate's long legs kept her within a stride of Colt as he rounded the corner. They practically ran into Tori, who crouched a couple of yards ahead. She was hunkered down behind a bush, her gaze on something they couldn't see.

Kate scooted to a stop next to her friend, then dropped to her knees. "Are you nuts?" She whispered the words through gritted teeth. "Why'd you come here after you heard that awful cry?"

Tori simply pointed but didn't say a word.

Kate and Colt looked, and Kate's mouth dropped open.

The old woman stood over a freshly dug grave, her body quivering and her arms full of something the size of a child, wrapped in an old blanket. She slowly knelt and placed the bundle in the hole. Then another unearthly wail rent the air.

Colt gripped Kate's shoulder with one hand and Tori's with the other and hissed in their ears, "Let's get out of here. Do you see that grave marker? It has a name on it!"

Kate's body froze as she looked where he pointed. A white cross was driven into the ground at the far end of the hole, and she could clearly see one word: *Sam.*

As the three of them edged backward, the old woman stood with the help of a shovel that was sunk in the ground beside her. Then she grasped the handle, pulled the shovel out, and tossed a shovelful of dirt into the hole. She lifted her fist to the air and shook it at the heavens, then let loose another long cry.

Even Tori's body started to quiver as she retreated from her position behind the bush and made her way around the corner of the house. "Wow."

"No kidding." Colt dusted off the knees of his jeans. "That was creepy. I kept thinking of what Melissa said about somebody disappearing years ago, and the ol' lady burying them here."

Kate picked up her bike and straddled it. "The bundle she put in the grave was about the size of my little brother." She shivered and rubbed her hands together. "Totally creepy, if you ask me. We'd better get out of here."

"Right." Colt pushed his bike a few yards up the driveway, then swung aboard, with Tori following.

"Hey!" A quavering voice rang out from behind them.

All three of them stopped. Kate was afraid to look back, but she did. The old lady stood there, shaking her fist in the air. "I told you kids not to come here again, and if you know what's good for you, you'll leave me in peace. I can't take any more, do you hear me?"

Tori gasped and stood on her pedals, then shot ahead of Kate and Colt. Kate didn't hesitate. She followed as close as she could, happy to hear the crunch of Colt's tires on the gravel behind her but unable to shut out the ongoing rant of the old lady, who stood next to the fenced-in flowerbed that now seemed like something out of a science-fiction movie.

Kate skidded to a stop beside Tori, where they'd met Colt less than an hour earlier, and worked to calm her breathing. "I'm never going back there again, Tori, no matter how much you beg me to."

Tori's lips quivered. "Me either. That was scary."

Colt nodded. "Although I'd sure like to sneak in there sometime and dig up that grave and see what she buried—or who." His eyes sparkled with mischief, and he held up his hand in mock surrender when the girls moaned. "Just kidding. I don't think she buried a person, but I don't get why she was crying and screaming. Or why she came after us. It's not like we had anything to do with whatever died."

Tori scuffed her toe against the gravel. "So what now? Go home and forget all about it? Do we tell Melissa?"

"I don't think we should," Kate said. "Even though she said she didn't want to come back, she might get mad that we didn't invite her. I'm not crazy about being enemies again."

Tori glanced at Kate. "How about our parents? What do we tell them?"

Colt's eyes widened. "Your parents don't know you came? I mean, I didn't tell mine, since you called and it was a big rush to get here, but I left my mom a note telling her I was going for a bike ride and would be home soon."

"We told our mothers that we were coming here to bring cookies, but we haven't told them about the rifle or her chasing us off. We figured they'd be upset about it, and they might not have let us come today."

Colt grunted. "You think?"

Tori stiffened. "Did *you* tell your parents about her waving a rifle in the air?"

"Well, not exactly. I told them we found out where she lived and accidentally upset her when we came in the wrong way, and she told us to leave." His face reddened. "Sorry for the sarcasm."

Tori relaxed. "And I'm sorry for getting mad. I guess I'm upset at everything that's happened."

"But it's mostly our fault," Kate said. "She never asked us to come on her property and bug her. We've done it twice now, even after she made it clear the first time that she didn't want us there. So we can't be mad at her."

"But I wanted to be nice! That's why I suggested we bring cookies and apologize. It's not like we knew we'd upset her. Besides, she's the one who scared us, not the other way around."

Colt rocked his bike back and forth. "Maybe, but we don't know that for sure. What if she isn't crazy, and we did scare her?"

Kate remembered the old lady gently placing the bundle in the grave and shivered. "But she buried something that died. How do we know it wasn't a person? You know, a little kid or something?"

"I doubt it," Colt said. "I'll admit she was kinda scary when she ran around the house screaming, but we don't know what was actually going on."

Tori gripped her handlebars tighter. "Let's go home. Whatever her deal is, I don't want to go there again, no matter how sorry I feel for her or how much I love her horse."

Kate woke to the sound of the doorbell the next morning. Why didn't Mom answer it? She glanced at the clock and groaned. Only eight o'clock—she'd stayed up so late last night worrying that she didn't feel like she'd slept at all. Mom was probably out throwing hay to the horses they were boarding, and Dad had already left for work.

She swung her feet over the edge of the bed. No way could she get dressed before whoever it was gave up and left. Most people knew to check the barn, though, so they'd probably find Mom.

She took a quick shower, then tugged on her jeans, shirt, and socks. A glance in the mirror was all it took to scrape her curly hair into a ponytail before she headed down the stairs. Swinging open the front door, she peered toward the barn, even though she didn't expect to see anyone after all this time. Kate stepped back and glanced down. An envelope with a small rock on top lay on the mat. She picked it up and examined it, but there was nothing written on either side.

Should she open it or go find her mom? As much as she wanted to tear into it and see what it contained, it probably wasn't for her. She stuffed it in her jeans pocket and headed for the barn. Time to help with the feeding and stalls anyway.

She walked through the open door of the alleyway that fronted the indoor arena, flanked on each side by a long row of stalls. Capri, her chestnut mare, nickered at her but barely raised her head from the rack of hay.

Kate laughed, then slid open the door and stepped inside. "Ignoring me, huh? I'll come back when you're done to turn you out and clean your stall. Maybe I can get a ride in today. Would you like that?" Capri shifted from one hoof to the other, and her head seemed to bob. Of course, she may have simply been plunging her nose deeper into the sweet-smelling hay.

Kate left the stall and walked down the long aisle. "Hey, Mom? Where are you? Sorry I didn't get out sooner to help."

Her mother poked her head out of the office and smiled. "That's okay, sweetie. I'm almost done. I kind of enjoy coming out by myself when Pete's sleeping so I can have a few quiet moments with the horses. It reminds me of all the hours I spent on the farm helping your grandpa. You ready to get to work?"

"Sure, but I wanted to give you something first. The doorbell woke me, but I couldn't get dressed and downstairs fast enough. Whoever it was had already left, but I found this on the doormat." She stepped into the office and plucked the envelope out of her pocket, then handed it to her mom. "I figured it must be for you or Dad, so I didn't open it."

Her mom gave her an approving smile. "Good girl." She turned to toss it on the desk.

"Hey!" Kate stepped closer. "I'm curious who left it. I mean, it's always possible it *might* be for me."

"Right." Her mom chuckled and tweaked Kate's ponytail. "Well then, I guess we'll take a look." She slid her finger under the flap that appeared to barely be glued and pulled out a single sheet of paper. She flipped it over and read the signature, then frowned. "I have no idea who Martha Maynard is, do you?"

Kate shook her head. "Nope. But if you read it, you might find out." She bounced on her toes, itching to take the paper and find out for herself. "Come on, Mom. Please?"

"Oh. Right." Mom bent her head and read silently, then looked up. "This isn't to me; it's to you. I think. Or maybe to you and Tori and Colt, at the very least. What's going on?" She planted one hand on her hip and frowned.

Kate groaned. "I have no idea. May I read it?" She held out her hand and waited. "I mean, if it's for me, I'd like to see it."

Her mother reluctantly handed it over, her forehead still creased. "Read it, and then I expect a full explanation."

Kate bent her head over the letter, noting the beautiful, flowing script. She didn't know anyone wrote like that anymore. She'd seen letters that her grandmother had written as a young woman to her grandpa, and they were similar. Pushing those thoughts aside, she concentrated on the contents.

My dear young people,

My name is Martha Maynard, and I believe I owe you all an apology. After you left yesterday, I found your cookies and kind letter of apology for trespassing and startling me. I must tell you that I thought you four children were the hoodlums who have been throwing eggs at my mailbox and more recently at my house. I decided I'd had enough, and the first time you came through my back pasture and approached my home, I assumed you had come to cause more trouble. That's why I pulled out my rifle and waved it in the air. Please be assured it was not loaded, and I regretted my actions as soon as I lifted it in the air and yelled at you.

Then, an hour before you arrived yesterday, those same teenagers returned, driving a pickup down my driveway and shouting things about the crazy woman who lives here. My dog, Sam, ran out to chase them off, and when the kids backed up to leave, they hit him. He was an old, arthritic dog who wasn't long for this world, but I loved him dearly, and he didn't deserve to die like that. I chased them off and brought him in the house, but he was already gone.

When you came, I was saying my final good-bye and burying him in the yard that he loved and guarded for so many years. He was my best friend, and I wanted to give him a proper burial. I'm sorry you heard me wailing and carrying on. I was dealing with both anger and grief, and for a few minutes, I couldn't contain myself.

As I stepped around the corner and saw you three there on your bikes, I immediately assumed you were my tormentors come back to cause more havoc. As soon as I shouted at you and you started to ride away, I realized you were far too young to drive a vehicle, and you must have been the same children who came the day before. I especially remember the compassion on the face of the girl with the dark brown hair, and her kind words about my horse. I liked the

*looks of that girl as soon as I saw her, but I already had my rifle
raised in my hand.*

*I hope you'll forgive an old woman and allow me to make it
up to you. If you'd care to return, I'd like to make you some tea
and cookies and show you my Sam's grave. I'll understand if you
don't care to come, or if you'd like to bring your parents. I know the
children in this area think I'm crazy or a murderer, but believe me,
that is far from the truth.*

*With humble apologies and a hope that you might give me
another chance,*

Martha Maynard

Kate lifted damp eyes and met her mother's gaze. "Wow."

"You can say that again. Now you get on the phone and ask
your friends to come over here. I want to know exactly what's
going on. We're going to get to the bottom of this."

Kate froze. "Melissa too? Or just Tori and Colt?"

"Was Melissa with you when you went to this woman's
home?" Mom's stare didn't waver.

"Uh … the first time. But she didn't go with us yesterday."

Mom gave a firm nod. "Then she comes too. I've finished
feeding the horses, and the rest of the stalls can wait. I want
answers."

Chapter Ten

Kate looked around the room at her three friends. Then her gaze stopped briefly on Tori's mom before moving on to her own mother, who held the letter in her hands. Pete sat in the middle of the living-room floor, intent on working an intricate, one-hundred-piece puzzle that he loved putting together.

Her mom glanced at Tori's mother, Maria Velasquez. "Do you have any questions, Maria?"

The woman adjusted her petite body in the overstuffed chair. "Why are we only hearing about this woman now?"

Tori bit her lip. "We told you, Mom. Remember, I said I was coming over to Kate's to bake cookies for an old lady up the road?"

Kate's heart thudded at the disapproval on her mother's face. Melissa and Colt were lucky that their moms hadn't decided to come. "That's right. And Mom, you knew it was the woman who's been riding past our house on the black horse, and we'd been trying to find out who she was for days. It's not like we were keeping all that from you."

Mom lifted the letter in the air and waved it. "But you somehow forgot the little detail about that same woman waving a rifle at you and chasing you off her property, not to mention that three of you went back the very next day."

Melissa looked as if she was trying to hide a satisfied smile, but Kate still caught a glimpse of it. She must be feeling happy right now that she hadn't wanted to return after that first trip. Kate gritted her teeth. It was so not fair that she and Tori were the ones their moms were pointing their fingers at. She shifted uncomfortably and tried to ignore Melissa. "But she says in her letter that the rifle wasn't even loaded, and she felt terrible about it."

"She does say that, but you didn't know it at the time. What if it had been loaded, and she'd decided to take a shot at you? Even if she'd only been trying to scare you, the gun could have gone off, and any one of you could have been hurt."

Kate huffed. "But it wasn't loaded, Mom. And she didn't hurt us. She said she was sorry for scaring us."

Mrs. Velasquez leaned forward. "I'm more concerned that you kids didn't tell us the truth. You kept things from us."

"You're right," Colt declared. "We all should have told our parents, whether we only went once or twice." He didn't look at

Melissa, but Kate could have hugged him for his comment. "We felt bad that we kept it from you, but we wanted to apologize, and we weren't sure you'd let us if you knew the whole story."

Mom's posture relaxed a little, but she kept her gaze fixed on Kate. "Is that right, Kate?"

"Um, yes. Tori and I even talked about telling you, but we didn't feel like we were lying. We told you where we were going and why—to take the cookies to Mrs. Maynard. We just didn't tell you everything that happened the day before." She hung her head. "I'm so sorry. I guess I knew it was wrong when I made the decision, but I wanted to help."

Tori sprang to her feet. "I made the decision, Kate, not you. I said I'd go alone if no one wanted to go with me, and you only came to protect me. Then Colt agreed to come because he's our friend and was worried we'd do something stupid."

Kate chanced a look at Melissa, who was staring straight ahead, her face resembling a stone mask.

Tori leaned forward. "Melissa, we didn't ask you because you said you never wanted to go again. We weren't going to ask Colt either, because I figured Mrs. Maynard would be spooked if four kids showed up. But Kate called him anyway, 'cause she thought it would be better to have a guy along in case anything went wrong." She sucked in a deep breath. "We weren't trying to leave you out, really. And Mom, I'm so sorry I didn't tell you everything. It all happened so fast, and we didn't get hurt or anything, and we wanted to make it right."

Kate's mom raised her brows at Tori's mom, and something seemed to pass between them. Nan Ferris gave a quick nod. "All right, then. Here's what we're going to do. We're all going over to see Mrs. Maynard. You will apologize again for trespassing on her property and scaring her; then you'll thank her for her gracious letter, and we'll leave and never bother her again. Agreed?" She slowly looked from Kate to Tori to Colt and then stopped at Melissa. "Melissa, I realize you didn't go the second time, so I won't insist you come with us, unless you want to."

Melissa didn't even hesitate. "Only if they want me." She tipped her head toward Kate and her friends. "I'm not going where I'm not wanted." Her voice had an edge to it, and a little sneer tipped the corner of her lips.

Kate wanted to roll her eyes, but she didn't. Melissa was playing the sympathy card big-time, and Kate bet she was loving every minute of it. It felt as though they were starting over at the beginning. "Of course you can come. Like Tori said, we weren't trying to leave you out." She peeked at her mother and noticed a slight frown. "Uh … and we're sorry if you felt like we were. Come with us, okay?"

Melissa finally met her eyes, but the arrogance she'd expected wasn't there—only what appeared to be genuine longing.

Kate didn't get it. Half the time Melissa was nice and acted like she wanted to be friends. Then suddenly she was sneering and smirking again. Kate wanted to be nice and act like a Christian, but sometimes Melissa made it hard. Then all of a sudden, she'd get that puppy-dog look—all sad and lonely—and Kate didn't know what to think. She sighed. "So, you coming with us or not?"

Twenty minutes later, Kate sat in the backseat of her parents' Subaru Outback, wishing she could have ridden with Tori, Mrs. Velasquez, and Colt. Instead she got stuck with Melissa, who sat in the front seat, while she and Pete ended up in the back. "We should have tried to call Mrs. Maynard before we barged over here, Mom. She's probably going to freak."

Her mom opened the door and swung her legs out. "I couldn't find a phone number for her, and she invited us to come. I assume she'd expect us to show up not long after she delivered the letter."

Tori's mom parked her car behind them, and everyone got out. Mom had parked partway down the driveway, and they could see the house not far ahead.

"What now?" Kate asked.

"We go up and knock on the door like civilized people." Her mom waited for Mrs. Velasquez to step up beside her. Then they headed to the house.

Kate's stomach jolted like it contained a hive of angry bees. Would Mrs. Maynard be the woman who shouted at them and chased them off, or the one who had written the letter? She bumped Tori's shoulder as they walked. "Is your mom still mad?"

Tori shrugged. "Not as much as she was earlier, but I'll probably be grounded if Mrs. Maynard gets upset again."

Colt and Melissa drew alongside, and Colt's normal happy attitude seemed to be missing. "Guess we blew it, huh?"

Melissa glanced at him, then at Kate and Tori. "I still don't get why you guys wanted to come back after I told you the old lady was crazy."

Kate stiffened. "Did she sound crazy in the letter Mom read? I think people have gossiped about her for so many years, they've forgotten she's a nice person."

Melissa huffed. "She didn't act nice the day we were here."

Kate couldn't help it. She blurted out what she was thinking. "Then why did you agree to come today if you still think she's crazy? You heard my mom—no one was going to make you."

"I dunno. I guess it's better than sitting around at home while my mom watches TV and drinks wine all day."

Tori's eyes widened. "She does what? Seriously? I mean, hey, I'm sorry."

Melissa scuffed her feet on the gravel as she slowed her pace. "I shouldn't have said that. Forget it, okay?"

Colt nodded. "Yep. We didn't hear a thing. Right, girls?"

Kate and Tori exchanged a glance, then both replied, "Right."

Tori's mom led the way through the gate in the picket fence, and Kate's mom smiled at the color surrounding them. "This is lovely. Mrs. Maynard has quite a green thumb. I wish I could create something like this at our house." She stopped to lean over a rose and sniffed. "Nice. So many roses don't have fragrance anymore."

Some of the tension drained from Kate at her mom's peaceful expression. If only Mrs. Maynard wouldn't come out waving a gun.

Chapter Eleven

Kate slumped in relief after Mrs. Velasquez knocked twice with no reply. They weren't going to have to face Mrs. Maynard's wrath after all—assuming she'd changed back into the person she'd been when they were here last. Kate swiveled and then headed down the porch stairs. "Come on, she's not home. Let's go."

Tori caught up with her and grabbed her wrist. "Hold it. Remember last time she was in the back, burying her poor dog. Maybe she's there again and can't hear us knock." She looked at her mom. "She invited us." She pointed toward where they'd seen Mrs. Maynard burying her dog. "Shouldn't we at least walk around the house and check?"

Kate couldn't believe it—and right when they were about to make an escape. "Last time we were here, you said you never wanted to come back. Now you want to check behind the house? What's with you, Tori?"

Colt stopped beside them. "Sorry, Kate, but I agree with Tori. If we don't find Mrs. Maynard today, we'll have to come another time if we're going to make things right."

Kate's mom headed for the gate. "It can't hurt to check. Kate, please keep an eye on Pete." She strode toward the corner of the house and rounded it, Tori's mom on her heels.

Melissa stared after them. "What happens if they don't come back?" she muttered. "I don't care what that letter says. I still think that old lady is crazy. She could have made all that stuff up, and it wasn't a dog she was burying." She glared at Kate.

Pete started to whimper and rock, and Kate glowered at Melissa. "Knock it off. You're scaring Pete. Mom believed that letter, and so does Tori's mom. You can walk home if you don't want to be here, but we're staying."

Melissa's eyes widened and she knelt in front of Kate's brother. "I'm so sorry, little guy." She dropped her voice to a whisper. "But you guys never should have come back yesterday. If you'd listened to me, this wouldn't be happening, and your mom wouldn't be in danger."

Tori and Colt moved closer to Kate.

"I think you're freaked out for nothing, Melissa." Colt leaned down in front of Pete. "It's okay. Your mom went to talk to a nice lady, and she'll be back soon. Right, Kate?"

Kate squatted on her heels. She wanted to wrap her arms around her little brother and give him a hug, but she knew he wouldn't allow it. "Hey, buddy, Colt's right. And you never know. The lady might even have M&M's."

Pete's eyes darted to her face for a second, then shifted to the far corner of the house where his mother had disappeared. "Want Mama, not M&M's."

"I know. She'll be back soon, I promise." Kate prayed that was true—her little brother so rarely showed a need for anyone. She bit her lip. Why had she allowed Melissa to get to her? Why did she agree to let Melissa be part of their group when she knew what kind of person she'd always been?

But was that fair? Not long ago, she'd felt that God had brought Melissa into their group for a reason. Maybe she should wait and see what happened before making a judgment.

Mrs. Velasquez appeared at the corner of the house and beckoned. "Come on, kids. Mrs. Maynard asked me to get you."

Colt and Tori moved forward, but Melissa hung back, her eyes wide.

Kate stopped beside her. "What's up? Are you coming?"

Melissa shook her head. "I'm scared."

That was the last thing Kate expected to hear. She thought Melissa had been hassling them about Mrs. Maynard being crazy simply to cause trouble. "She's not going to hurt us. Tori's mom wouldn't have told us to come if she was dangerous."

Sweat broke out on Melissa's forehead. "What if she still has that rifle?" She whispered the words, then took a step toward the car.

Kate reached out her hand. "Come on. I'll walk with you. She's just an old lady." As soon as she said the words, she knew they were true. How silly she'd been to worry. "You heard what she said in her letter, and I don't think she was lying."

Melissa stared at Kate's hand, then edged forward. "All right. But I'm outta here if anything goes wrong, and you guys will be on your own."

Kate stifled a laugh. "Works for me. We'd better hurry before they get out of sight."

Melissa bolted forward as though hit with lightning. "I don't want to be alone!"

Kate followed behind her at a jog as Melissa rushed toward the corner where the others had disappeared. As soon as they reached the backyard, Kate drew to a stop by Tori, unsure of what was happening.

She peered around the run-down area, wondering why this was so different from the front with all the beautiful flowers. Most of the yard was hard-packed dirt, with an occasional shrub, patch of grass, or green plant, but there was no sign that anyone had put much effort into landscaping. As she remembered, the covered porch was in terrible shape, with the screen door open and hanging on its hinges, and several of the shingles loose or missing. But there wasn't a scrap of litter or garbage in sight. Even though it was bare and almost ugly, it was neat and clean, as if someone had taken pains to tidy the area for company.

Kate leaned close to Tori and whispered, "What's going on?"

Tori pointed, and Kate's gaze followed her finger. Mrs. Maynard stood by the new grave, her head bowed and her shoulders shaking.

Kate's mother stood beside her. She slipped her arm around the older woman and drew her close. "I'm so sorry. I know how hard it is to lose someone or something you love. His name was Sam?"

Mrs. Maynard swiped at her cheeks with the back of her hand. "Yes. He was my friend, and the best dog I've ever had. I didn't own him. You can't own an animal, you know. If they give you their heart, then you're simply taking care of them for God while they live out their life. Sam gave me his heart when he was a puppy, and I gave him mine. I miss him so much." The last word ended with a sob. "Thank you for coming. I had no one to share this with, and I'm grateful."

Mrs. Velasquez patted her shoulder. "We're glad you invited us. I think our children have something they'd like to say." She turned. "Tori, Kate, would you come over here?"

Kate glanced at Tori. "Sure." She tucked her hand into the crook of Tori's elbow, feeling the need of a little support, and Colt followed.

Tori drew in a deep breath. "Mrs. Maynard, we're so sorry we upset you when we came. We were only curious about your beautiful horse and why you were riding at night."

The older lady raised her head and stared at Tori, and it was all Kate could do not to gasp. A horrible scar ran from the outside of her eyebrow all the way down her face and under her chin. It looked as if someone had taken a jagged knife and slashed her face. Kate raised her hand and touched her own cheek. Whatever caused that must have hurt terribly.

Melissa gave a little shriek and backed up a step, but Colt caught her by the wrist and whispered something Kate couldn't hear. Melissa stopped in her tracks and bowed her head.

Mrs. Maynard gave a gentle smile. "I didn't realize you children hadn't seen my face before—I'm sorry for startling you. That's why I ride in the evening with the cloak and the hood. I got tired of explaining or putting up with frightened stares and whispers from children and even adults. I know that's part of the reason for some of the rumors over the years. That and the fact that I prefer to stay close to home and don't go out more than I must."

"But what happened?" Kate blurted the words before she'd even realized they'd formed in her thoughts.

"Kate!" Her mother frowned. "That was rude. Please tell Mrs. Maynard you're sorry."

The older woman shook her head. "No need. She only asked what I'm sure all of you are wondering. Won't you come sit while I bring some iced tea?" She gestured toward a tree off to the side, not far from the pen where the black gelding paced. She took a step toward Pete and gingerly lowered herself to his level. "What's your name?"

"Pete. What's your name?" He lifted blue eyes and met hers for a moment before they shifted away. "Do you have M&M's?"

"It's very nice to meet you, Pete. My name is Martha. I don't have any M&M's, but if you come visit me again sometime with your sister or mother, I'll be sure to have some. How does that sound?"

"Good. Can I pet the cat?" He pointed at a cat curled up in the sun not far away.

"I'm sure Milton would like that. He's a very friendly cat, and he thinks I don't give him enough attention. Can you be very gentle with him?"

He nodded, then wandered over and sat on the grass by the cat.

Kate noticed six wicker chairs and a little table sitting on the only patch of grass in the area. "That's pretty. And your front yard is beautiful."

"Thank you, dear. I was starting on this, but I got sick a few months ago and didn't have the energy to continue. It's as much as I can do to keep the flowerbeds watered and exercise Starlight occasionally."

"Starlight?" Tori breathed the word. "Is that your horse? He's so beautiful."

"Yes. You probably didn't notice when you were here before or when we rode by, but he has a tiny spot of white on his forehead about the size of a silver dollar—the only white on his body—and it's shaped something like a star. He's a good boy, but he's getting mighty restless since I haven't been able to ride him as much as I used to." She motioned to Colt. "Would you help me bring out a tray with glasses and iced tea?"

He nodded, then followed her to the back porch, reappearing a few minutes later with a heavily laden tray.

Kate sank into one of the chairs. "If you used to ride him a lot, why have we only seen you this summer?"

Tori giggled. "Silly. You moved here a few months ago, remember? And none of our houses are on the same road where Mrs. Maynard lives."

"Oh. Right." So much had happened since Kate's family had moved to Odell that it seemed as though she'd lived here a lot longer than a few months.

Colt served the drinks, then settled onto the grass so Mrs. Maynard could have a chair.

She seated herself and took a long drink, then set her glass on the round table. "I'm sorry I startled you today, and that I scared you the other two times you came. As I explained in my letter, I thought you were the teens who have been bothering me—that is, until I found your cookies and note. If you'd be willing to humor an old woman and listen, I'll tell you my story."

Kate's mom nodded. "It's not a bother at all. We'd be honored to listen if you'd care to share."

"Thank you. It's not a long story, and I'm not complaining, simply stating facts. Many years ago, when I was a few years older than you girls"—she nodded at Kate, Tori, and Melissa—"I was considered quite pretty, but I didn't care about boys or clothes or the things most girls craved. All I cared about was horses."

Melissa quit fidgeting in her chair, and Tori leaned forward.

Kate smiled. "That's how all of us kids feel, even Colt." She giggled. "What I mean is he doesn't care about clothes or boys— uh, I mean girls—and he likes horses too." Warmth crept into her cheeks as Colt burst into laughter. "Sorry for interrupting, Mrs. Maynard."

"It's fine, dear. I don't mind at all." She smiled at Tori. "And I thought that might be the case after I read Victoria's letter."

Tori's brows rose. "How did you know my real name?"

"Your mother told me when I complimented her on the lovely note her daughter had written. She said that her Victoria has always been good with words, and I have to agree." She waved a wrinkled hand in the air. "Now back to my story. When I was seventeen, I was a princess in the Fort Dalles Rodeo, and I was crowned queen. I was so excited that after the coronation and the parade, I went out with my friends to celebrate. The young man who was driving had been drinking, but none of us worried about it. At that age, we thought we were invincible— especially me, after I'd won the crown. I felt everything in my life was going my way."

She took a sip from her glass, then set it back down. "But all of that changed when he ran a red light, and a pickup smashed into the side of our car."

Chapter Twelve

Kate gasped. "What happened? How badly were you hurt?"

Mrs. Maynard's eyelids fluttered. "A big piece of jagged glass hit my face and tore it open, and my leg and ribs were broken. But I was lucky. My best friend, who was in the backseat with me, was killed. The boy who was driving walked away with only a broken arm, but the other boy in the front had a severe head injury and was in a coma for over a month. All because we didn't see a problem with having a few drinks to help us celebrate." She shook her head. "If only we could go back and make better decisions for our lives … but that's not possible."

"What happened then?" Tori barely breathed the question.

"They didn't have the type of reconstructive surgery back then that is available today. There was a lot of broken glass in my face wound, and it tore through muscles, not just the flesh. The doctor did the best he could at our small hospital, but my parents didn't have the money for a specialist who might have done better. That accident changed my life. The boy I was dating broke up with me when he saw my scar, and I was unable to complete my responsibilities as rodeo queen, due to my injuries. The emotional scars I carried as a result of the accident, and how ugly it left me, made me a recluse in my own home." A tear trickled down her wrinkled cheek.

Melissa's face contorted. "But that's terrible. How did you stand it? I would have wanted to die."

"That's how I felt for a long time. It took months for the wound to heal, and even longer before the red started to fade. My ribs and leg healed, but I was broken inside. My parents urged me to see my old friends, but I didn't want to, and my friends eventually quit calling or coming by. When they'd visited in the hospital, I saw the horror and pity in their eyes. I didn't want anyone's pity, and I wouldn't be an object of ridicule. So I cut them off, believing it was best for them and for me."

Melissa nodded. "I understand."

Kate blinked, suddenly realizing what Melissa must have been feeling. When her friends found out Melissa's family wasn't rich like they'd believed, Melissa must have faced those same reactions. She'd pulled inward and cut herself off from them rather than deal with the whispers and gossip. What kind of courage had it taken for Melissa to come to the barn the day they were painting the fence and take the chance the three of them wouldn't reject her as well?

Kate wasn't sure she could have done it, and new respect rose in her heart for Melissa. All Melissa's cutting remarks were probably to cover up her own fear and pain. From now on, she was going to be kind to Melissa, no matter how snotty she acted. Kate had a feeling it might take Melissa a while to trust their friendship, but she was determined to prove it was real.

And poor Mrs. Maynard. Kate couldn't imagine what she must have gone through—being crowned rodeo queen, then losing it all due to someone who'd been drinking. She shuddered, remembering what her parents had always taught her about being responsible and making good choices. That made even more sense now that she'd heard Mrs. Maynard's story.

Melissa's gaze stayed fixed on Mrs. Maynard, as though she was trying to discover something important. "So you didn't leave the house the rest of your life? That must have been awful."

"No, dear. Only that first year. Then one day my parents convinced me to attend church with them again. The pastor had visited faithfully since my accident, and not once did I see disgust or pity when he looked at me, so I decided to go. I told my parents I'd sit in the back, and if one person gasped or sneered, I'd leave and never come back."

"What happened?" Colt asked.

She drew in a long, slow breath as though remembering, then released it with a soft sigh. "A few people greeted me and told me they'd been praying for me, and others simply nodded and smiled. But one young man came over, grasped my hands, and stared right into my eyes, not even noticing my face. He said that God had placed me on his heart from the time he'd heard about the accident, and he'd been praying daily ever since. He introduced himself as Joshua Maynard." She gave them a warm smile. "And I'm guessing you can figure out the rest of the story."

Melissa relaxed in her chair, all the tension seeming to drain from her. "You married him."

Mrs. Maynard chuckled. "Not right away. It took me months before I trusted him enough to go out with him, and another couple of years before he convinced me my scars didn't matter— that he loved me for who I was, not what I looked like. Besides, he said he thought I was beautiful, and that's all that mattered. He saw into my heart and loved what he saw, and I loved him for it until the day he died ten years ago, and I still do."

Tori swiped at her eyes. "That's cool. But I don't understand why you don't want to come out of your house now."

"I'm tired, dear. And most of my old friends have moved or died or gone to an old folks' home. The new people don't know my story, and I get tired of dealing with the stares. I still don't care for pity, and sometimes it's easier to stay home with Sam,

Starlight, and Milton." Her face clouded over. "That is, until Sam died. I'm lonelier than I expected."

Melissa got up, went to the older lady's side, and knelt in the grass by her chair. "I'd like to come visit you again, if that's all right?"

The story Mrs. Maynard told must have really touched Melissa, Kate thought, startled. "I want to come too."

Colt nodded. "I was thinking if you're not feeling well, we could help with your yard work. I'm pretty good at planting stuff and hauling bark chips, and I'll bet the girls wouldn't mind doing a little housework, or whatever else you need."

Tori bounced in her seat. "I'd love to exercise Starlight—I don't mean ride him—but I could take him out of his pen on walks or lunge him. I'm good at that." She suddenly wilted. "If Mom agrees."

Mrs. Velasquez smiled. "It's a nice thought, but we don't want to impose on Mrs. Maynard."

The older lady looked from one to the other. "Goodness! It wouldn't be imposing. I'd love if the children came to visit again, although they certainly don't need to do work. Tori, if you'd like to go make friends with Starlight, feel free. But don't enter his pen. He's not partial to strangers."

Kate squeezed her lips together to keep from giggling at Mrs. Maynard's use of *children.* Of course, at Mrs. Maynard's age, even a nineteen-year-old might seem like a child, much less a bunch of thirteen-year-olds. "I'll help wherever you need me. It's not like we have much planned for the summer."

Melissa groaned. "Except for that parade, and we still don't have any banners for our horses."

Colt sighed. "Maybe we should ditch the idea."

Mrs. Maynard's brows rose. "What's this about a parade?"

Kate opened her mouth to answer, then thought of Melissa. She had brought up the subject, and she was supposed to be the head of their committee. Maybe letting Melissa answer would show a bit of trust. She tipped her head. "Melissa is the head of our parade committee."

Melissa straightened, and her face brightened. "We were pumped when we first talked about the idea, but it hasn't come together like we'd hoped. Kate and her family own a boarding stable where we all keep our horses."

Tori swiveled and stopped her advance toward the nearby corral. "All except me. I mean, I don't have my own horse. I use Mr. Gray, the lesson horse at the barn. He's really sweet." She tossed a longing look at Starlight. "But he's not near as pretty as your horse."

Mrs. Maynard's face crinkled in a wide smile. "He's special, that's for sure," she called as Tori continued toward the corral. Then the older woman turned to Melissa. "You said something about banners for the horses. Is that what you meant by things not coming together?"

"Yes. We'd like to advertise the barn by riding our horses and having nice banners over their rumps, but we're not sure how to come up with the money for the fabric or what we should wear."

"I see." She rested her head against the back of her chair and closed her eyes.

Kate's mom pushed to her feet. "I think we need to go. We don't want to tire you."

"No, no." Mrs. Maynard opened her eyes. "Let's check on the girl who's so interested in my horse. Tori, I believe her name is." She took her time rising and shook her head when Colt stepped near and offered his hand. "I'm fine, young man, but thank you. The doctor says I should rest, but I also need a certain amount of exercise to keep my joints limber."

She walked at a slow pace toward the corral, with Kate's and Tori's mothers following behind a ways. Tori leaned on the fence, her hand outstretched to the black gelding. Starlight nuzzled her palm and nickered. "My goodness, how unusual. Starlight doesn't like many people. In fact, he never comes near a stranger, and sometimes I have trouble catching him. He must sense something special about you."

Tori's cheeks flushed, but she kept her gaze on the horse. "*He's* the special one. As soon as I whispered his name, he came up to me."

"Has he allowed you to touch him?" Mrs. Maynard squinted at Tori.

"Yes. I stroked his face, but I think he's expecting a treat."

"I wouldn't be surprised. I'm afraid I've spoiled him."

"How old is he? Have you had him all his life?"

"He's fourteen, and yes, I owned his mother and raised Starlight from birth. He's the smartest and kindest horse I've ever owned, but like I said, he doesn't take to many people. Never has. I had a trainer come once, and she had a dickens of a time catching him. Then he refused to budge when she got on, and she even laid her spurs into his side." She shook her head and clucked. "I'd told her not to wear them, but she wouldn't listen. Thought she knew best."

Kate moved up beside them. "What happened?"

Mrs. Maynard gurgled a laugh. "He didn't hurt her, if that's what you're asking. But he did a lot of dancing, along with a couple of crow hops that convinced her she didn't want to stay on long. The trainer told me I'd misled her when I said he was broke to ride, and she didn't care to work with a horse that was green and ill mannered. I told her he was completely broke, but he didn't like spurs or a rough hand. She didn't return. Starlight and I didn't care." She crooned to the horse and stroked his face.

Melissa strolled over and climbed on the rails, then held out her hand. "Hey, Starlight. Can I pet you too?"

The horse shied and snorted.

Colt chuckled and leaned against a rail several feet from Melissa. "Don't feel bad. I bet he won't come for me either." He reached through the rails and clucked his tongue. "Come on, boy. We're not going to hurt you."

Fascinated, Kate watched as Starlight shook his head and pawed the dirt. She wasn't going to try. Apparently this horse had decided he liked Mrs. Maynard and Tori, and that was it. But she was thankful Colt had tried, or Melissa might have felt like she'd been rejected again—even if it was only a horse.

The last thing Kate wanted was Melissa being jealous of Tori and causing trouble for her friend. She planned to continue to be kind to Melissa and help her feel a part of their group, but there was no way she'd put up with her taking out her frustration on Tori. She was probably the kindest girl Kate knew, and Tori didn't deserve that.

Mrs. Maynard gave Tori an approving look. "He likes you, young lady. Would you care to groom him for me? I'm afraid I've neglected him of late—at least, I haven't spent the time I usually do since I've been sick."

Kate held her breath. Tori had always been afraid of strange horses, but she'd offered to exercise Starlight.

Tori nodded eagerly. "Yes, ma'am, I'd like that." She turned to her mother, who stood nearby. "Is it okay, Mom?"

Kate knew Tori was remembering what a difficult time they'd had convincing Mrs. Velasquez to allow Tori to work at Mountain View Equestrian Center a few months ago. Tori had come a long way with the riding lessons she'd taken at that barn, then at the Ferrises', and Kate couldn't have been more proud of her friend.

Mrs. Velasquez paused, looking uncomfortable. "I suppose, if Mrs. Maynard says her horse is safe, and he's tied up or someone is holding him. I don't want you in the pen with him loose, though."

Mrs. Maynard took a halter and rope off a nail on a post, then swung open the gate. Starlight gave a gentle nicker and moved toward her, his body relaxed and his head extended. She slipped the halter on and secured it, then led him to the fence and tied the rope to the top rail.

The next several minutes were spent gathering the grooming tools, then Tori went to work, crooning over the black gelding as she brushed out his mane. "You're a beautiful boy. Did you know that? I'll bet you're the smartest horse in the county, if not the entire state."

Melissa rolled her eyes. "Now that might be taking it a little too far." She glanced at Mrs. Maynard. "No offense meant, ma'am."

The older lady smiled. "None taken, but I have to agree with Tori. Starlight is the smartest horse I've ever met, and I've been around plenty in my almost seventy years." She looked at Colt. "Young man, would you mind staying here with Tori? I have something to do inside, and I'd like Kate and Melissa to accompany me."

She peered at Kate and then Melissa, and her voice dropped to a husky whisper. "That is, if you aren't worried I'll kidnap you or bury you in my basement."

Chapter Thirteen

Melissa shivered and rubbed her hands on her arms, then glanced at Kate, who gave her a huge grin and a wink.

Kate couldn't believe Melissa had fallen for Mrs. Maynard's joke, but Melissa was the one who'd believed all the gossip to the point she'd refused to return, until they received the letter.

Melissa glared at Kate, then swung toward Mrs. Maynard. "Are you making fun of me?"

"Why no, dear. But I've heard the rumors and know what many of the children and teens in this town think. I thought you'd appreciate my attempt at humor. I'm sorry if it frightened you. If Kate's willing to come, you're more than welcome to stay with your friends. Or one of the ladies can accompany me instead, if anyone is concerned about it being suitable for you girls."

Kate's mother chuckled. "I'm not a bit worried. Kate can go if she'd like to, and Melissa, please do stay with us if you'd rather."

Kate grinned. "I'd love to." Her smile faded as she saw uncertainty flash across Melissa's face. She held out her hand. "Come on. I want you along, Melissa."

The girl's lips formed a little O. "Really? Cool! I mean … sure, I suppose it isn't a big deal."

Mrs. Maynard gave an approving nod. "Since that's settled"—she glanced at Tori—"will you and Colt be all right? You don't feel left out, I hope."

Colt draped an arm over the paddock rail. "I'm good. I'm guessing it's gonna be girl stuff anyway, so I'll hang out with the horse. And Tori," he said, almost as an afterthought.

Tori huffed, then giggled. "I guess I can't be mad at that, since I'd rather hang out with Starlight than you, Colt."

"Ouch! You wounded my pride."

"Whatever." Tori waved him away, then turned her attention to Starlight.

Kate's mom beckoned to Mrs. Velasquez. "Let's go sit in the shade where we can keep an eye on Pete—he's quite taken with Mrs. Maynard's cat. It would be nice to get out of this hot sun, and we can see the kids from the chairs. Besides, I think there's a little iced tea left in the pitcher." She led the way to the tree where the wicker chairs were placed.

Kate looped her hand through Melissa's arm. "Let's go. Mrs. Maynard is already halfway to the house."

"Right." Melissa moved in time with Kate's step, then lowered her voice. "What do you think she's up to?"

Kate slanted a look at the girl. "You don't trust her?"

"I'm not sure. She seems nice enough, and I guess she was telling the truth about burying her dog, but why does she only want the two of us to come in her house?" She shivered. "It's strange, that's all."

Kate quickened her pace as Mrs. Maynard held open the porch door and waited. "I guess we'll find out soon enough!"

Mrs. Maynard allowed them to enter the house, and she followed. Kate blinked, waiting for her eyes to adjust to the dim light. She glanced around, taking in her surroundings. It wasn't at all what she'd expected. But she wasn't sure exactly what she'd expected. A dump? A dingy mess that stank like garbage, or worse? "This is awesome!" She breathed the words and moved toward a glassed-in display of photos and trophies. "What are these from?"

Mrs. Maynard stepped close. "Those were taken of me during high school when I was showing horses and competing at barrel racing. That was my first love. I always thought I'd reach nationals one day, until I was in the accident."

Melissa gulped. "Why would you give that up? Did your broken leg keep you from competing?"

"Yes, for a while. But mostly I simply gave up." She tapped her chest. "In here." Then she pointed at her head. "And mostly in here. I was convinced I would never amount to anything, due to this horrible scar. So I kept to myself and quit trying."

Melissa stared at the photos. "You were beautiful." She breathed the words as though saying a prayer. "I had no idea." An instant later, she put her hand over her mouth. "I'm so sorry. I didn't mean it like that."

Mrs. Maynard shook her head. "It's all right, dear. I'm too old now to care whether I kept my beauty or not, but back then, I thought I'd lost my entire world."

Melissa glanced at her. "So going to church fixed everything?"

"Oh no. Not at all. Church can't fix anything that's wrong in the world. It can give a helping hand and show compassion, but true change and help only come from the Lord. He's the one who heals the brokenhearted and restores hope." She peered at Melissa. "I see you don't know that for yourself, do you?"

Melissa ducked her head. "I dunno. Kate's told me a little about it, but it's all so new—and strange."

"Yes, I imagine it would be. Give it time, Melissa. And keep your heart open. If you ask God to show Himself to you, He will. Of that I am certain." She smiled and pointed toward the far side of the tidy living room that oozed comfort and warmth. "I need to go upstairs. Will you girls accompany me?"

"Sure." Kate fell in behind Mrs. Maynard, then looked back at Melissa. "You coming?"

"Uh. Yeah. I guess." Melissa darted a wary look at the dark staircase, then made a face. "Sorry. I'm being stupid." In two long strides, she caught up with Kate and the older woman. "I can't wait to see what you want to show us."

Apprehension slithered through Kate as Mrs. Maynard stopped at the base of a dark, narrow staircase when they reached the second floor. Silly. She shouldn't have been listening to Melissa's nonsense. But why would Mrs. Maynard take them up to the attic? "Are we going up there? Do we need a flashlight?"

"Certainly not." Mrs. Maynard flipped a switch on the wall. "I had electricity wired in the attic two decades ago."

Melissa exhaled loudly. "Good. I'll admit I'm not crazy about dark places where there might be spiders."

"I don't blame you, and that's why I keep this handy as well." She plucked a flyswatter off a nail next to the switch. "Now that we're armed with light and a weapon, let's go."

Kate giggled, envisioning the older woman marching into battle armed only with a flyswatter as a giant spider dangled overhead. Then she sobered, wondering how far that might be from the truth. "What's up there?" She hated that her voice shook the tiniest bit, but she couldn't help it.

Melissa grasped Kate's hand. "Yeah. That's what I was wondering."

"You'll see if you're patient. I think you'll be happy you trusted me once we're upstairs." She trudged up the stairs and swung the door open at the top. A musty odor drifted out. "Are you girls coming?"

The two girls looked at each other, and Kate gave a brief nod. "All right. Let's go."

They trooped up the stairs after Mrs. Maynard, but they didn't let go of each other's hands. Kate hoped they'd made the right decision trusting this woman. Of course, their mothers were right outside, and Mrs. Maynard was small, so what did they have to be afraid of?

Chapter Fourteen

A dim light sent some of the darkness scurrying into the corners, but deep shadows still lingered in the low-ceilinged room. Melissa stepped through the doorway behind her, and Kate could feel her breathing on the back of her neck. Not that she blamed her. This place was spooky.

Mrs. Maynard gave her a smile, but in the wavering light, it didn't look warm or inviting. "What's wrong, girls? Have you already seen a spider?"

Melissa pressed closer to Kate's side. "It kind of gives me the creeps up here."

"I'm so sorry, dear. We needn't stay long." Mrs. Maynard shuffled to a corner, where the dim glow from the single overhead bulb barely reached. "Would one of you be so kind as to pull this box out for me? I'm afraid it's a bit more than I should attempt."

Kate stared at the box she could hardly see, then glanced at Melissa. Wide-eyed Melissa shook her head. Kate moved forward. "Is it heavy?"

"Not terribly, but it's hard for me to bend over very far. I'm sorry to have to bother you with this." Her tone was gentle and helped ease some of Kate's fears.

"Sure." Kate took three strides and reached the box. She bent over and tugged, and it moved easily under her hands. "It's not heavy at all." She nudged it again and pushed it into the middle of the room. "But it's covered with dust. Should we take it downstairs?"

"Hmm." Mrs. Maynard pursed her lips. "I suppose that might be best. I'd planned to open it here, but I didn't realize how dusty everything would be. Will it be a problem for you to carry it down?"

Relief flooded through Kate at the thought of leaving the dark attic. She could fly down those steps with a box twice this heavy and not be bothered. "Nope. Want to go now?" She plucked the box off the floor and held it against her chest.

"Certainly, dear. Why don't you lead the way?" Mrs. Maynard waited for Kate and Melissa to precede her, then turned off the attic light and closed the door.

Kate shivered as the door thumped, thankful she was no longer in that creepy place. She bolted down the stairs and walked into the living area. "Where would you like me to put this?"

Mrs. Maynard led the way to a pine coffee table and patted the top. "Right here is fine. Then you and Melissa take a seat on the couch while I open it." She frowned as Kate set it down. "I'll get something to dust the top with first."

She returned in a moment and swiped the top of the box with a damp cloth. "Much better. Now, let's see if things are still in good shape. If so, we'll have to go back up and get another box. But I didn't see any sense in that if these are moth- or mouse-eaten."

"Ugh." Melissa wrinkled her nose. "I don't think I want to go back up with moths, mice, *and* spiders. I thought seeing a spider was bad enough."

Kate wasn't afraid of bugs, but she agreed. All she wanted to do was get back outside with Tori and Colt. They probably thought they were missing out, but *they* were the lucky ones in the sunshine with a gorgeous horse—instead of being trapped in a spooky house.

Mrs. Maynard didn't respond, but she peeled off the wide band of yellowed tape that covered the line where the flaps met.

Kate peered closely at the box. It didn't appear to be nibbled, so maybe the contents were safe. She almost wished they wouldn't be, so she and Melissa wouldn't have to venture upstairs again. "What's inside?" She leaned forward and kept her gaze fixed on the box as Mrs. Maynard carefully pulled back the top.

Melissa hitched forward onto the edge of her seat. "Oh my! What a beautiful cherry-red color! Is that satin?"

"Yes, it certainly is. You have a good eye, Melissa." Mrs. Maynard slipped her hand under the folds of fabric and withdrew a good-sized swath. "What do you think?"

"It smells musty, but it's a pretty color," Kate agreed. "What's it good for?"

Mrs. Maynard laughed. "I suppose I should open it." She stepped away from the coffee table and unfolded the satin to its full width, longer than her opened arm span. "Now can you see it?"

Kate gasped. "Where did you get that? I can't believe it!" She stared at a gorgeous banner that was the perfect size and fit to go over the back of a horse. The words Fort Dalles Rodeo Princess Court were emblazoned in black letters on each side. "Wow!"

Mrs. Maynard smiled. "I have three more. And the letters can easily be unstitched and new ones added to say whatever you'd like. If you children would care to use them for the parade, that is."

Melissa gaped at her. "You mean after all the things we did to upset you, you'd let us use these? Why would you do that?"

"They aren't doing me any good in my attic, are they? And who better to use my old things than four children who want to take their first ride in a parade? It would make me feel like I had a small part in your barn and your lives, and maybe even like I was riding in a parade again myself." She swiped her fingers beneath one eye and sniffed. "Forgive a foolish old woman for getting sentimental. This banner brings back memories."

Kate shook her head. "That's very kind of you, but it would destroy those memories if we took the letters off and put new ones on. That wouldn't be right."

"I don't agree," Mrs. Maynard said. "It would be wrong to let them stay in that attic, where creatures can eat holes in them. It's a wonder this is still intact. We'll have to hope the rest are in as good a shape, since there are only four. Are you girls willing to go up again and get the rest of the boxes? There are three more, one for each horse, as I didn't want to carry a large box up the stairs."

Kate and Melissa jumped to their feet, all fear gone about going upstairs.

"Sure. Come on, Melissa. Those boxes are small enough that one of us can carry two. Why don't you stay here and rest, Mrs. Maynard? Are the other boxes in the same area, and may we use your flashlight?"

"Yes, they're right behind where we found this one." She handed over the light and settled herself in an easy chair. "I *am* a little tired after all the excitement and exercise, but it's good for me. I've been so lonely. You girls let me know when you're finished. Feel free to open the boxes and check the banners when you return. I'll just rest my eyes for a few moments." She shut her eyes and tipped her head against the overstuffed chair.

Kate grabbed Melissa's hand and raced to the stairs, her heart thudding in her chest. She waited until they were halfway up before she whispered to Melissa, "Here all this time we've been worried about having the money to buy nice fabric and get it sewn to fit a horse, and God hands it to us! Wow!"

"What do you mean by that? God didn't do anything. Mrs. Maynard did." Melissa stayed close behind Kate and crossed the threshold into the attic a half second after Kate flipped the light switch.

Kate walked toward the corner where they'd found the box and turned on the flashlight. "Don't you think it's pretty weird that we'd see an old lady riding a horse by my house close to dark, then find out where she lives, and after we do, we discover she used to be a rodeo queen and has what we need for the parade? I mean, what are the odds of that happening? As far as I'm concerned, God brought it all together, and it's awesome!"

Melissa peered into the dark corner and pulled out a box the same size as the first one. "But why would He do that?"

"Because He loves us, silly."

Melissa shook her head. "Maybe you, but not me. I've never done anything to make Him love me. You're a nice person—you and Tori and Colt all are—but I haven't been. I guess He did it for you guys." Her shoulders drooped.

"Nope." Kate grabbed the corner of another box and tugged it into the light. "Not true. I think He did it to show you that you're important to Him."

"It's just too weird. Although I'll admit it would be amazing to have somebody love you so much that He cares about stuff that's important to you." She gave a wistful sigh as she retrieved the final box. "We'd probably better get downstairs before Mrs. Maynard starts worrying about us."

Melissa picked up one box, and Kate grabbed another. "Hmm," Melissa said, "I'm not sure we can balance two of these and go down the stairs safely. Why don't you wait here with the flashlight, and I'll take this one, then come back and get the other one, and we'll take the last two down together. Okay?"

Kate nodded. "Sure. You'd better be quiet, though, in case Mrs. Maynard is asleep. I guess you can put the box on the table with the other one."

"Right." Melissa headed to the door and disappeared.

Kate waited as the seconds turned into minutes, and Melissa didn't return. She stepped to the door and shone her light down, even though the stairwell was already lit from the single bulb hanging overhead. "Melissa? Where are you?" she whispered as loudly as she could, hoping her voice would carry, but no foot-steps echoed below.

Suddenly a scream bounced from the living area all the way up the stairwell. Kate dropped the box and ran down the stairs. Melissa's frantic voice met her as she hit the bottom step.

"Kate, Mrs. Maynard is dead!"

Chapter Fifteen

Two hours later, Kate and her mother, Colt, Melissa, and Tori and her mother stood in a room at Providence Memorial Hospital in Hood River, where Mrs. Maynard lay tucked in a bed, her small frame not even filling half of the narrow surface.

A doctor patted her hand. "Your friends can stay another ten minutes. Then I want you to sleep. You're lucky it was only a mild stroke. I'll release you in a few days if you improve, but you need at least three or four weeks of rest before you try to do much at home. I'll be back in a couple of hours to check on you. Call the nurse if you need anything." He exited the room without looking back.

Kate edged closer to the bed as another wave of relief swept over her that their new friend wasn't dead. Finding Mrs. Maynard slumped in the chair and not being able to wake her had brought Melissa to tears and near hysteria. "What can we do to help?"

Mrs. Maynard gave a weak smile. "You are all so wonderful to offer. First, I want you girls to get the boxes you brought down from the attic. Those banners are yours to use as you'd like to. Now that Sam is dead, it's just my cat, Milton, and Starlight. Could you see that they're fed every day? And Tori, would you continue to brush Starlight and exercise him like you offered until I can get home?"

Tori swiped at a tear rolling down her cheek. "Yes, ma'am. I'd love to. Would you like me to lunge him in his pen?"

"Hmm … I was thinking … Do you girls have a trainer you trust?"

Kate looked at her mother, who nodded. "We have a lady who comes to our barn and gives lessons, both private and group, a couple of times a week. She's really good."

"That's what we need, then. Mrs. Velasquez, would you allow Tori to take lessons on Starlight, since Mrs. Ferris trusts the trainer? I'd like you to take him to Kate's barn until I'm well enough to care for him again. I'll pay for the trainer and his board, if that's acceptable. Joshua and I had a special little nest egg set aside for emergencies, but we never spent it … Now seems like the perfect time."

Tori stared at Mrs. Maynard, then swung her gaze to her mother. "Please, Mom? He's a sweet, wonderful horse. I promise I'll do everything the trainer tells me to, and I won't do anything silly."

Mrs. Velasquez paused, then asked Kate's mom, "What do you think?"

"Our trainer is very competent and careful. She can assess Starlight when he arrives and decide if it's safe for Tori to ride him. If not, Tori can work him from the ground."

"I'll agree to that. Tori, I know you love this horse, but I'll hold you to your promise to follow the trainer's instructions."

Tori looked like she wanted to jump up and down and whoop, but she merely grinned. "Absolutely. Thanks, Mom. And thank you for trusting me with your horse, Mrs. Maynard. I won't let you down."

"Thank you, dear." The older woman rolled her head on the pillow and closed her eyes. "I think I'd better rest now. I seem to be quite tired all of a sudden."

Kate's mom squeezed Mrs. Maynard's hand and leaned close. "We'll be praying for you. And I want you to know that I alerted the police about the teens who have been harassing you. They're going to keep an eye on your place." She straightened, then beckoned to Kate and her friends to follow.

Colt was the last one to leave, and he closed the door behind him. "I feel sorry for her. I wonder if she'll ever be able to live at home by herself again."

Melissa sucked in a long breath and then released it. "I'm thankful she's alive and can talk. I was so scared when I found her unconscious. The doctor said she'll be able to go home if she gets stronger, but she can't do much on her own anytime soon. How will she take care of herself?"

Kate looked at Tori, who gave a slow nod as though she knew exactly what Kate was thinking. "I say we take turns bringing food and cleaning her house. It's not like one person who's in bed or on the couch most of the time will mess it up, but we can do her dishes and vacuum—stuff like that—and water her flowers."

Colt stuffed his hands in his pockets as they made their way down the hall to the front door. "Count me in. I'll do the yard work if you girls bring food and clean. Tori has Starlight's care, so she probably won't have time to do much at Mrs. Maynard's house."

"Sure I will. It's summer vacation, and it's not like I have a job. I'll do my share."

Kate stood by the automatic door and waited for everyone to exit into the parking lot before following. "It's so exciting that you get to work with Starlight. We'll need to find someone to trailer him to the barn right away."

Tori arched her brows. "Why? It's only a little over a mile. If you guys come with me, we could walk him there."

Her mother shook her head. "You aren't handling that horse without an adult present, until the trainer says it's safe."

Tori sighed. "Right. I forgot."

Kate's mom pressed the remote and unlocked their Subaru Outback. After they were all inside, she turned to Mrs. Velasquez. "I'm willing to stop by Mrs. Maynard's on the way home and walk with the girls, if you'll take my car on to my house."

Tori squealed from the backseat, and Kate elbowed her. They didn't want to push Tori's mom and have her change her mind. Tori sobered and hunkered into the seat, but her expression remained hopeful.

"All right." Tori's mom nodded. She turned to look at Tori. "But you are not to do anything with that horse until the trainer arrives. Understood?"

"Sure. Besides, he'll need a day to settle into his new surroundings, and the trainer comes tomorrow, right, Kate?"

"Right. And Melissa, we should probably get to work on those banners right away too. The parade isn't that far off, so we don't have a lot of time."

This was so cool and exciting. They had banners, and Tori got to care for Mrs. Maynard's horse. Poor lady. Kate had seen the loneliness on Mrs. Maynard's face more than once. It was so sad that a nice lady like her didn't have a bunch of friends to keep her company and care for her. Of course, she said most of her friends were dead or had moved from the area. Then reality hit her. Mrs. Maynard was getting old—or at least, she said she was seventy, and that sounded old to her. What if she had another stroke and died, or could never care for her house or animals again?

Chapter Sixteen

Five days passed before Mrs. Maynard was released from the hospital. Kate, Tori, and Colt, along with Kate's mom, picked her up from the hospital. Kate could barely believe the change—Mrs. Maynard was so much stronger and more energetic than the last time she'd seen her.

They helped her into the front seat of the Subaru, but she waved away the robe the nurse wanted to tuck around her. "It's eighty degrees outside. I'll melt or have another stroke from the heat. I'm fine. I'm just happy to be going home. That's all I need." She bestowed a warm smile on the nurse, who stood beside the open door, the wheelchair a few feet away. "Thank you for all you did for me while I was here."

The nurse leaned down and squeezed Mrs. Maynard's hand. "You take care of yourself. We don't want to see you back here anytime soon."

"That I will, my dear … That I will."

The nurse shut the door, and Kate's mom started the car. She eased it out of the parking lot and headed down the hill, then smiled at Mrs. Maynard. "We'll have you home shortly, but you tell us if you're uncomfortable or need anything on the way."

"I'll be right as rain as soon as I get home and have Milton on my lap. Tori, how are things going with Starlight?"

"Great!" Tori bounced in her seat between Kate and Colt as Kate's mom drove through downtown Hood River. "I've been grooming him every day, and I've ridden him three times now! The first two with the trainer there, and the last time with Mrs. Ferris, 'cause Mom trusts her to watch me while I ride. Starlight is the smoothest, gentlest horse I've ever ridden. I love Mr. Gray, but Starlight is even better. He's an awesome horse!"

Kate's mom smiled but kept her eyes on the road as she turned right onto Highway 35. "Tori is a natural with Starlight. And he responds to her better than for me or the trainer. He's very smart, and he seems to know what Tori wants him to do almost before she asks."

Mrs. Maynard nodded. "When he's in tune with a person, that's how he is—he anticipates and is ready to please. I'm so glad he took to you, Tori. It makes me feel much better about not having him at home right now." She sighed. "The doctor says I can't care for him for a few more weeks. He's afraid too much exertion might cause more problems, and he wants me to build up my strength slowly. Is it going to be all right if Starlight stays at your barn longer than I planned?"

"It's fine if he stays, but it's up to Tori if she wants to continue working with him." Kate's mom glanced in the rearview mirror at Tori.

"Cool! I'd love to." Tori beamed. "But I'm sorry the doctor won't let you do much. I promise I'll love Starlight and take care of him like he was my own. I'll brush him every day, exercise him, and feed him carrots—and anything else you want me to do." She gave a happy sigh. "I love Starlight."

"And how about the parade? Did you children get the banners finished?"

Kate leaned forward. "Yes. I wish Melissa could have come today and told you about it. Her mom has a friend who agreed to sew on the new letters after we cut them out. It says Blue Ribbon Barn, Odell, Oregon, on each side now. We named it after Melissa won the silver spurs and blue ribbon at the show this summer. We decided white would show up best against the cherry-red background. They look great! We'll bring one over to show you if you'd like. Oh, and I'm afraid we might have spoiled your kitty with treats. I hope he won't be too much of a pest."

Mrs. Maynard chuckled. "Milton has always been a pest when it comes to treats or being petted, but I love him just the same. I doubt you did too much damage." She glanced out the side window. "It looks like we're almost home. It will be nice to sleep in my own bed again and not have someone coming in poking and prodding and waking me up."

"I kept your flowers watered, and the girls weeded and did housework. If there's anything we need to do different, we'll take care of it," Colt said.

"You children are so kind to an old lady. I don't know what I'd have done if you hadn't come along."

Kate shivered as the memory rushed back of Mrs. Maynard slumped in her chair with her eyes closed and barely breathing. She'd been so sure the older woman was dead, and the image had given her nightmares for several nights, until Dad came in to pray with her. "One of us will come over every day to see you and take care of your yard and house for as long as you need us to."

"Right," Tori added. "And I'll give you a report on Starlight. Do you think you can come to the parade and watch us ride? We'd love to have you see our horses dressed up in the banners you gave us. I'm riding Mr. Gray, and he's going to look great in red."

They pulled into Mrs. Maynard's drive, and Kate's mom parked the car. Her cell rang, and she frowned. "Sorry, guys, it's our trainer, so I'd better take this." She answered, then listened for a moment. "He did what? Oh no. Are you sure? Right. I'll be home as soon as I can."

Kate pushed open the door and hopped out as her mother exited the front seat. "What's going on? It's not Pete, is it? His tutor is there, isn't she?"

"No, it's not Pete." She glanced at Tori, who now stood by Kate. "Mr. Gray has pulled up lame. We need to get Mrs. Maynard settled and go see how bad it is."

Mrs. Maynard opened her car door and struggled to step out.

Colt bolted around the rear of the car and reached her before she could swing her feet onto the ground. "Hey, you shouldn't be walking on your own yet." He put his hand out and helped her to her feet, then turned to Kate. "You guys go with your mom. It's not that far to my house from here. I can walk. But I'll get Mrs. Maynard settled and call you later to see how Mr. Gray is doing. Sure hope it's nothing serious."

Tori's lips quivered. "Do you know what happened?"

Kate's mom shook her head. "Only that he pulled up lame while a student was jumping him, so it could be a stressed tendon. We'll have to wait for the vet to find out. He can't be ridden for now, and I'm guessing it might be a while before he's cleared, if it's as bad as the trainer thinks."

Kate gasped. "Oh no! You mean Tori might not be able to ride in the parade? That would ruin the whole thing. All four of us have to ride, Mom. It's important!"

Mom leveled a stern gaze at Kate. "I know it's important, but so is Mr. Gray's health. We can't ask him to do something that could make him worse, or lame him for life. You wouldn't want that, would you?"

"Of course not, but this is awful!" Kate looked at Tori, who seemed to be fighting tears.

"Colt, thank you for taking care of Mrs. Maynard." She smiled at the older woman. "We'll come over later and check on you. Please call if you need anything." Kate's mom climbed back into their car. "Hurry up, girls. The sooner we find out the extent of the injury, the better."

Kate stood with Tori a short distance from Mr. Gray as Dr. Alan ran his hand down the gelding's leg and pinched his tendon, causing the horse to lift his foot. The veterinarian clamped a tool to the hoof wall close to the heel and pressed. "This final test will give me a little more information." He held it for several seconds, then removed the tool and set the hoof back on the ground. "Walk him and then trot him in a straight line away from me."

He watched as Kate's mom followed his instructions, then turned Mr. Gray and brought him back. "Good. He's no worse than before. So far every test indicates it's not navicular, and from what I'm seeing, I think he may have popped a splint."

Tori wrinkled her nose. "He did what?"

Dr. Alan ran his hand down the inside of the long bone between the horse's knee and his fetlock joint. "The average person might think of the fetlock joint as an ankle, and this, of course, is his knee. The bone between is the cannon bone, but there are small bones on the inside of the leg called splint bones that help support the cannon bone. A horse can fracture one of those. If you run your hand down his leg you'll feel quite a bit of heat, so the area is inflamed. There's also a very small bump that could get larger."

Tori bit her lip. "Will he be lame forever?"

"Not with proper rest." He turned to Kate's mother. "You'll need to keep him in his stall, put an ice pack on it for at least thirty minutes twice a day, and he'll need to wear a support bandage the rest of the time. A light massage of that area could also be beneficial, if you have time."

She nodded. "How long will he need to be stalled and not ridden?"

"I'll take another look at him in ten days. Hopefully the inflammation will be gone by then. If so, I'd say another three weeks before he can have light work. Once the inflammation is gone, there's no need for the ice, but someone will need to walk him for fifteen to twenty minutes a day until he's sound again. Thankfully, this appears to be a mild injury, but it could still be thirty days or so before he's under saddle again, depending on how quickly he heals."

"Thank you, Doctor. I have vet wrap and ice packs on hand, so we'll get that started this evening."

Kate beckoned for Tori to follow her. They opened the half gate and stepped into the alleyway that divided the indoor arena from the long row of stalls. "I'm glad he's not permanently lame, but it sounds like we can't use Mr. Gray for the parade." She kicked at a clump of dirt on the rubber mat under her feet.

Tori's bottom lip trembled, and her eyes watered. "I guess I'll watch from the sidelines this year. I can at least be your cheering section." She worked to muster a smile but didn't quite make it.

"I'm not going to give up that easily, Tori. Somehow we'll find a way for you to ride with us. Who knows? Maybe one of our boarders would let you ride their horse."

Tori shook her head. "No way. It could cause problems for the barn if something happened to the horse during the parade. Besides, I wouldn't feel safe on a strange horse like I do on Mr. Gray. The thought of riding *him* in the parade was all I could handle."

Kate was torn between getting mad and crying. Just when they had their banners all made, they were finally friends with

Melissa, and they'd solved the mystery of the horse and rider, this had to happen. She hated that Tori would be left out of the excitement and fun. Somehow Kate had to figure out a solution to this problem. "Come on. Let's call Colt and Melissa and see if they have any ideas."

Tori gave a halfhearted shrug, but she followed Kate from the barn, her head bent and her shoulders heaving.

Chapter Seventeen

Ten days later, Kate stood at the half wall of their indoor arena beside Mrs. Maynard. She kept her voice low so Tori wouldn't hear, although the chance of that with Tori in the center of the ring was slim. "She's doing well, don't you think?"

"I do." The older woman leaned on a cane but wasn't as stooped as she'd been when they first met her. She seemed to have blossomed since Kate and her friends had been taking turns visiting and helping at her house. "But I'm not surprised. Starlight is beautifully trained and will respond to a rider he trusts. I could tell that Tori won his heart as soon as she spoke to him. There's something about that girl …"

Kate nodded. "She's one of the nicest people I know, and Starlight probably senses that."

"I'm sure that's true." She watched as Tori cantered the black gelding around the ring as their trainer called out instructions. "And you say she hasn't been riding long?" She peered at Kate over the wire-rimmed glasses she'd been wearing since she got out of the hospital.

"Only a few months. I've never seen her so confident, even on Mr. Gray." She sighed. "The inflammation is gone from his leg, and he's not limping anymore, but the vet says he still can't be ridden for at least three more weeks to be sure he doesn't hurt himself any worse. I feel so bad for Tori, but she's not upset anymore."

Mrs. Maynard didn't reply but kept her eyes on Tori as she pulled Starlight down to a trot.

"He looks so smooth," Kate said. "She said he's springy but not choppy, and it's easy to post on him. That's how my mare, Capri, is—she's a dream. I wish Tori could ride her in the parade, but she's afraid of her."

Mrs. Maynard turned her gaze on Kate. "And what would you ride, young lady, if Tori rode your Capri?"

Kate scuffed her foot on the ground. "I got to win a ribbon in the horse show, and I own Capri. Tori doesn't have her own horse. If she could ride Capri, I'd be happy to watch from the sidelines." She pressed her lips together. "Well, that's not totally true. I might not be happy for me, but I'd be awfully glad for Tori."

"That's the mark of a true friend—one who would give her life for another."

Kate scrunched her brows. "I didn't say I'd give my life for her—just my horse for the day."

Mrs. Maynard chuckled. "I'm sorry, dear. It was something from the Bible, that's all. I didn't mean it literally. I simply meant you are showing true love and friendship by being willing to make that sacrifice."

"Oh." Kate didn't know what else to say, so she turned her attention back to Tori. "Do you want to see the banners? Colt and Melissa should be here any minute. Melissa is bringing all four of them so we can try them on our horses. We thought we could put one on Mr. Gray and take a picture of him and Tori together, and then Mom is going to take one of all four of us and our horses."

"That would be very nice, thank you. I think I'll go inside and talk to your mother and rest while you children get ready. I'm a bit tired from standing so long. Please call me before you put the banner on Mr. Gray."

Curiosity pricked at Kate's mind, but she nodded. "Yes, ma'am. Do you want me to walk you to the house?"

"No, no. I'm fine. But don't forget to let me know when Colt and Melissa arrive and you have all the horses out and ready to blanket." She moved down the alleyway toward the house at a slow pace, humming a little tune as she shuffled along.

Kate and her friends finished brushing their horses, and Melissa patted Mocha's neck. Her black bay gelding had finally recovered from his own injury earlier in the summer. She turned to Kate. "I loved riding Capri, but it's sure nice to have my own horse again." She glanced at Tori, and a flush rose in her cheeks. "I'm sorry, Tori. I shouldn't have said that. I feel so bad that you can't ride Mr. Gray. I'll let you ride Mocha if you're willing."

Kate's heart swelled with joy. This was the first time Melissa had made such a completely unselfish offer in all the time Kate had known her.

"That's really nice of you, Melissa." Tori gave Melissa a shy smile.

Kate decided not to mention that she'd already said the same thing to Tori about Capri.

Melissa kicked at a clod of dirt. "Kate did the same for me, even when I'd been mean to her. Tori, you're the kindest person I know, and I'd like to do something nice for someone else for a change."

Colt set down his horse's hoof and dropped the hoof pick in the tack box by his feet. "Romeo's pretty gentle, and I've been in parades before, so you could use him if you're scared of Mocha or Capri."

Tori gazed from one to the other, her eyes brimming with tears. "You guys are the best. I've never had friends like the three of you before. But I'm not going to take any of your horses."

She stroked Starlight's neck, then pressed her face into his black mane. The horse nickered and nudged her, as though letting her know he returned the sentiment. "I'll watch from the sidelines with Mrs. Maynard. Really. I was kind of scared to ride in the parade anyway. Mr. Gray is great and everything, but I still don't feel as safe on him as I do on Starlight. I'm not sure why, since Mr. Gray has never done anything wrong."

Colt pulled one of the red banners out of a bag. "Guess we'd better get saddled."

Kate nodded. "I'll get Mrs. Maynard. She's resting in the house and visiting with Mom, but she asked that we call her when we're ready to put the banners on." She didn't wait for a reply but jogged up the aisle. Poor Tori. She was being so brave about not riding in the parade, but Kate could tell her friend was sad.

A few minutes later, Kate returned with her mom and Mrs. Maynard, walking slowly so the older woman could keep up. "The horses are groomed, and we're putting the banners and saddles on so Mom can take a picture. We're excited you let us use your banners, Mrs. Maynard. I'm not sure what we'd have done without them."

"You're welcome. I don't know how I'd have gotten along without the help of you and your friends." She waved a hand toward the row of four horses tied in front of each of their stalls. "Now that's a pretty sight, if you ask me."

Kate slipped past her and stopped in front of Capri. One of her friends had draped a banner over the arena half wall. She picked it up and carefully smoothed it over Capri's back, then placed the saddle pad and saddle on top of it as Colt, Tori, and Melissa did the same with theirs. "Wow! The red even shows at the bottom edge of the saddle, and the lettering on both sides in the back shows up perfectly. Blue Ribbon Barn. It's so awesome to see that in print!"

Tori finished buckling Mr. Gray's girth, then turned a troubled frown toward her friends. "You guys should be in the picture, not me. I'm not riding in the parade, so it's silly for me to be in the picture."

Kate started to protest, but Mrs. Maynard held up her hand. "May I say something?"

Kate nodded. "Sure."

Mrs. Maynard glanced at Kate's mom, who simply smiled. "Nan and I talked about this, then I called Tori's mother to discuss it as well. We're all in agreement that Tori should ride Starlight in the parade this Saturday. That is, if she wants to." She raised her brows and looked from one face to the next, ending with Tori's.

Kate gasped, but she didn't reply. This was Tori's surprise, and it had to be her decision. She only prayed that Tori wouldn't be too scared to ride the beautiful black horse.

Tori's jaw slacked and her lips parted. "Really? You trust me to ride him?"

"Yes, I certainly do. I've seen the way you treat him, and how responsive he is with you. I can't think of anyone I'd trust more than you."

"But what if I have an accident, and he gets hurt? I'd never forgive myself. I'm not an experienced rider, and I don't know what I'd do if anything happened."

Mrs. Maynard patted Tori's hand where it rested on Starlight's mane. "Let's take it one day at a time. Put the banner on Starlight and get the pictures taken, then you can ride him down the road with your friends. You'll get a feel for how he does with cars going past, and you'll be a lot less nervous about the parade."

Tori gave a slow nod, but Kate could still see the uncertainty and a glimmer of fear in her expression. "All right. We'll do that. Thank you for trusting me. I hope I won't disappoint you."

Chapter Eighteen

The day of the parade was hot and clear, with no breeze to break the stillness. Kate, Tori, Colt, and Melissa sat on their horses in the lineup, awaiting the signal to start. Kate couldn't believe the number of people swarming the streets and standing around the start area, not to mention the floats and other entries.

It wasn't anything like the huge Rose Festival parade they held in nearby Portland, Oregon, each year. There weren't any elaborate floats. Mostly flatbed trucks, decorated with ribbons and flowers, carrying kids dressed in costumes, along with clowns, other equestrian groups, decorated cars and pickups, a Boy Scout group, the high school's marching band, and even the rodeo queen and her court.

Kate's dad patted her leg as she sat on Capri. "Your mother and Pete are going to stay with Mrs. Maynard near the end of the parade route. Tori's and Colt's parents and Melissa's mom left to find places midway, but I'm going to walk the entire length with you kids in case you need help with anything." His brows were drawn together in the way Kate recognized when he was anxious.

Somehow it reassured her rather than scared her, and she reached down to squeeze his fingers. "I was kind of scared at first, but none of the horses are acting up. Colt and Melissa have both ridden in parades, so Tori will ride beside Melissa, and Colt is riding next to me, behind the two of them. We'll be fine."

The announcer signaled for the police car to start, followed by the lead car in the parade containing the mayor of The Dalles and the guest of honor. Kate grinned at her father. "You'd better get out of the way, Dad. Looks like we'll be leaving soon. I'm glad they put the horses near the end of the line and that noisy band at the front. It's nice having another horse group in front and behind too. It's almost like being on a big trail ride."

Her dad moved to the sidewalk and waited until their small group moved out; then he kept pace beside them.

When they'd covered a full block with nothing more exciting happening than a little boy running out to grab candy that was thrown, and his mother snatching him back before he fell in a pile of horse droppings, Kate grinned. If that was the worst that happened today, she'd go home happy.

"Tori, how you holding up?" She almost had to holler the words over the noise of the band three blocks ahead of them and the chatter of the crowd on both sides of the street. Most of the businesses fronting Second Street were closed, and the sidewalk was packed with people straining to see. Of course, the majority of these people were in town for the carnival and the rodeo later in the afternoon, but it was still awesome that so many of them wanted to watch the parade.

Tori twisted her head toward Kate, and she wasn't smiling. "I'm still kind of nervous, but Starlight isn't."

Melissa reached toward Tori with one hand, as if she wanted to reassure her, but she couldn't quite touch her. "You're doing great! Just relax and have fun."

It took at least thirty minutes to reach the end of the business district, even though it was only about six blocks long. Tori called back over her shoulder, "Are we almost done?"

Colt chuckled. "Nope. We're over halfway. We have to cross the railroad tracks and stop at a big pullout, although some of the entries will continue on a little farther to the rodeo grounds."

Kate stroked Capri's neck. "You're such a good girl," she crooned to her horse. "Hey, Colt. Why do you think Tori's still so nervous? Starlight acts like an old hand."

"Not sure. I guess because she hasn't had as much experience riding like the rest of us. It's a good thing we decided not to toss candy to the kids on the sidewalk."

Kate nodded. "This is tons of fun, but I don't think I'd have liked that either. I want to keep both hands on my reins. I've only ridden for less than a year longer than Tori."

They passed a lumberyard with a store adjoining it and saw Mrs. Maynard stand up next to her lawn chair and wave a hanky. "You children look wonderful!" Her voice carried over the thinner crowd, as most of the people had chosen to watch from downtown. Starlight pricked his ears and nickered in reply. "Keep up the good work!"

Kate's dad walked at a brisk pace beside them for the next four or five blocks. "We're almost there. We have to cross the tracks down a side road up ahead, then a short distance to where the horse trailer is parked."

Kate grinned. "It's a good thing you run so often, or you'd be wiped out by now, Dad."

"Yep." He waved, slowed and held up his phone. "I'll keep you in sight, but I want to see if Mrs. Maynard and your mother plan to head this way soon."

"Okay." Kate blew out her breath. "This has been great, but it'll be nice to be home." She looked at the line ahead of them, watching as entries crossed over the railroad tracks. It was a good thing no trains came through this time of day.

The group of horses and riders representing a local 4-H club crossed over the tracks. Melissa and Tori went next, and Melissa pointed ahead of them. "Watch out for that area where the two tracks come close together. You don't want Starlight to get a hoof caught in that crack."

Tori nodded and tightened her reins.

A child dashed out from the crowd, racing for the last handful of candy tossed out by the group in front of them, and she halted only a yard ahead of Starlight.

Kate's heart nearly stopped as Starlight got closer to the little girl.

Tori gasped and reined the gelding to the side to keep from running over the child, and a second later, the girl's mother snatched her into her arms.

Tori slumped in her saddle and relaxed her hold on the reins, then glanced back at Kate. "Whew. That was close. I'm glad we're almost done."

Melissa gestured ahead of them. "Watch it, Tori!"

Tori jerked her head around, but Kate could tell she wasn't sure what she was watching out for.

Kate groaned as Starlight's hoof plunged into the area between the two tracks and caught.

Chapter Nineteen

Melissa pulled Mocha to a stop, and Colt and Kate followed her lead. Kate dismounted as quickly as she could and looked around, hoping to see her dad. He'd said he'd keep them in sight, but he must have stayed on the phone a little longer than he'd planned. She turned to Colt. "What do we do?"

He dismounted, then handed her Romeo's reins. "Keep the horses calm. I'll see what it looks like." He moved forward calmly. "Good girl, Tori. Keep a tight rein on him. We don't want him trying to yank his foot out and hurting himself."

Tori swiveled her head, and Kate could see tears streaking her face. "I'm scared, Colt."

"I know. Keep talking to him and stroking his neck. Let him know he'll be okay, and you're here to help him. That will help keep him calm."

Tori nodded and bent over Starlight's neck. "Good boy." She ran her hand along his neck. "Nothing is going to happen to you, I promise. Don't move now, okay?"

Colt stepped up to the horse's head and grasped the reins close to the bit. "Get down slowly now, Tori, then come hold him while I see what I can do with his foot."

Tori did as he asked, slipping out of the saddle; then she walked forward and took Colt's place. "Is he hurt?"

Colt shook his head. "Not yet." He gritted his teeth. "I wish the rest of the entries would stop going around us. Kate or Melissa, do you think you can find Kate's dad?"

Melissa pivoted her horse. "Sure. I can see better from up here. I'll head back the way we came."

Kate stood to the side. "What can I do?"

Colt knelt beside Starlight but looked up at Kate. "Stand there with our horses. It's blocking anyone from getting too close to Starlight. Tori, you're doing a great job keeping him calm. Keep talking to him."

Just then a car pulled across the tracks and off to the side; then the back and front passenger doors opened, and Mrs. Maynard and Kate's dad and mom got out and headed their direction. Kate's hands shook with relief. "Am I glad you went back to get Mrs. Maynard, Dad. Starlight's foot is stuck."

Two men stopped and surveyed the scene. "Need help?" the taller one asked.

Mrs. Maynard took a moment to assess the situation with sharp eyes; then she gave a short nod. "Thanks, we might. But for now, we'll see what we can do. Tori, when I tell you to, put your hand over Starlight's nose, push backward very gently, and cluck to him. Colt, move slowly and put your hand on his shoulder. As soon as I say the word and you feel him start to shift, slide your hand to his fetlock and lift his foot, like you would if you were going to clean his hoof. Got that?"

Tori shivered but nodded. "Yes."

Colt put his hand on Starlight's shoulder. "Ready when you are."

Mrs. Maynard stepped closer. "Now, Tori, gently ease him back."

Tori didn't hesitate but slipped her hand over the gelding's nose and spoke to him softly, then clucked her tongue and pressed against the soft flesh.

Kate held her breath and waited, praying Colt would be able to extract the horse's foot.

As soon as the horse started to move, Colt slid his hand down Starlight's leg and lifted. The timing couldn't have been more perfect, as the hoof cleared the tight space between the tracks. Colt placed Starlight's hoof a foot back, and Tori kept up the pressure as the gelding walked backward.

A light cheer went up from the group, including the two men who had stopped to help and several other onlookers Kate hadn't noticed before. She grinned. "Thank You, Lord."

Melissa moved up to stand beside her. "Yeah. I agree. That could have been bad."

Kate stared at the girl, not sure if she'd heard correctly. "What do you mean?"

"I think God must have had something to do with Starlight staying calm and not breaking his leg. A lot of horses would have gone into a panic and tried to wrench their leg free. It wouldn't have been pretty."

Kate threw her arm around Melissa's shoulders and gave her a hug. "You've got that right. God even cares about horses. Pretty cool, huh!"

Melissa nodded and grinned.

With Colt's help, Tori led Starlight along the tracks to a place where it was safe to cross. Tori brushed her cheeks with the back of her hand.

Kate rushed to her friend. "You did great! I'm not sure I could have stayed calm if that had been Capri."

Tori shook her head and sniffed. She glanced over her shoulder at Mrs. Maynard and dropped her voice. "He could have been crippled because I wasn't paying attention. Melissa warned me to stay away from that side of the tracks, but after that little girl ran out in front of us, I forgot. It's my fault. I just know Mrs. Maynard is never going to want me to ride her horse again, and I won't blame her."

Two hours later, the horses were unloaded at the Blue Ribbon Barn, and the kids and adults were gathered in Kate's house. Her mom brought a tray of lemonade and glasses of ice into the living room, and Kate handed them around. When they finished, they both took seats on the couch, Kate settling in beside Tori.

Kate had been thinking about what Tori had said the entire time they loaded the horses and drove from The Dalles to Hood River and up to Odell. Would Mrs. Maynard blame Tori and not allow her to ride Starlight again? Kate didn't agree that it was Tori's fault and had tried to reassure her friend on the drive home, but she wouldn't listen.

Kate chanced a look at Mrs. Maynard, but she couldn't tell anything from the lack of expression on the older lady's face. At least she hadn't said anything negative, and she didn't look angry.

Tori's parents sat side by side on chairs near Kate's father. They'd come on the scene after Starlight was freed, but they'd heard the story more than once since.

Tori cleared her throat and looked across the room. "Mrs. Maynard, I'm so sorry about what happened. I know Starlight could have broken his leg, and I take full responsibility. I probably shouldn't ever ride him again, and I wouldn't blame you if you felt that way."

Mrs. Maynard's brows rose. "I don't remember saying that. In fact, I feel just the opposite."

Tori gripped her hands in a hard knot. "You do? But what do you mean *the opposite*?"

"That all of you children—no, young people—did a wonderful job today. Each of you did exactly what was needed and did it well. You kept your heads and didn't panic. And you, Tori …" She tilted her head. "In spite of your worry and fear, you were able to help Starlight relax. He trusted you to save him. I could see that as soon as I got out of that car. That's why I didn't come and take your place. Starlight was focused on your voice and your touch. I would have distracted him."

Tori's eyes widened, but she didn't reply. Kate could only imagine what she must be feeling right now, going from the certainty that she'd lost the use of her dream horse to being told she'd done well. Kate nudged her and grinned. "Way to go, Tori."

Mrs. Maynard smiled. "I agree. In fact, I'm glad we're all together right now, as I have something I need to share. I talked to my doctor yesterday. He informed me I'm not to ride again. Ever."

Gasps sounded among the kids, and several of them started asking questions. Mrs. Maynard held up her hand. "Give me a moment, and I'll explain. He's worried about what would happen if I'm riding and have another stroke. As much as I don't like it, I agree. I'm gaining strength every day, and I feel wonderful. But this body of mine isn't getting any younger. If I passed out and fell off Starlight, there's no telling what would happen to me or to him."

Tori slumped beside Kate, and Kate felt her shudder. "You're not going to sell Starlight, are you?" Tori almost whispered the words.

"Certainly not." Mrs. Maynard shook her head emphatically. "I'm going to give him away. He has years of riding ahead of him before he's old enough to retire, and it's not fair for him to live in a paddock getting hardly any exercise."

Tori fixed her eyes on Mrs. Maynard. "Where will he go? Can I still see him?"

Mrs. Maynard smiled. "I should have said I'm going to share ownership. I'll be giving him away, but I'll still own a part of him, so I can keep my visiting rights. I've spoken to your parents, and they've approved my decision." She looked directly at Tori. "Starlight will stay at the Blue Ribbon Barn, under your care, Tori. You and I will own him jointly. You'll ride and care for him, and I'll pay his expenses. I can't stand the thought of not being part of his life, so I hope that plan will suit you."

Tori squealed and lunged to her feet, then flew across the room and dropped to her knees beside Mrs. Maynard's chair. "Are you sure? Really?"

"Really." The older woman held out her arms.

Tori gently wrapped her arms around the slender body. "I love you, Mrs. Maynard. And not just because of Starlight." She drew back a few inches but kept her fingers wrapped around the woman's hand. "Because you have such a generous heart. I never even notice your scar anymore. God's love shines out of you all the time and makes you one of the most beautiful ladies I know."

A tear made its way down the weathered, wrinkled cheek. "Thank you, my dear. I will always bless the day the four of you appeared in my pasture. God is good. All the time."

Kate nodded and smiled at the group. "Our circle of friends used to be me, Tori, and Colt. But now that we've added Melissa and Mrs. Maynard, it's just about perfect."

Melissa bit her lip and looked like she was struggling between laughing and crying, but a smile won out. "Yeah. Thank you, guys. I think so too."

P.S.

... a little more ...

When a rockin' concert comes to an end,
the audience might cheer for an encore.
When a tasty meal comes to an end,
it's always nice to savor a bit of dessert.
When a great story comes to an end,
we think you may want to linger.
And so we offer ...

P.S. —just a little something more after
you have finished a David C Cook novel.
We invite you to stay awhile in the story.
Thanks for reading!

Turn the page for ...
- Secrets for Your Diary
- Kate and Tori's Chocolate Chip Coconut Oatmeal Cookies
- Author's Note
- Acknowledgments
- About the Author
- Sneak Peek at Book Four: *Blue Ribbon Trail Ride*
- Books by Miralee Ferrell

Secrets for Your Diary

Secret #1

Do you really think mean people can change and become nice people ... even friends?

Kate struggles with whether or not to believe Melissa Tolbert can change. After all, Melissa's the wealthy girl who has dissed and been condescending to Kate and Tori at school and while boarding at the Ferrises' barn. So why is she now offering to help paint the paddock fence and agreeing to work with them on ideas to promote the Ferris barn at The Dalles parade? Can Kate trust Melissa? What if she's only playing a game of being nice so she can embarrass Kate, Tori, and Colt later?

If you were Kate, would you choose to trust and include Melissa in your group? Why or why not? What would your friends tell you to do? How is this similar to or different from what Tori and Colt are telling Kate?

Note from Kate

At first I didn't want to give Melissa a chance. She'd been mean to me and Tori, and I figured she'd always be the same. I'm so glad that

Colt and Tori encouraged me to accept Melissa and not be so quick to judge her. I guess God has really blessed me—He gave me friends who love me and don't dump me just because I'm not the richest or most popular girl in school. I know He wants me to give other kids the same gift of friendship, and with His help, I'm going to try to do that from now on.

Secret #2

Have you ever been burned by somebody who seemed to be nice to your face but then talked about you behind your back? How did that gossip make you feel?

Kate, Colt, and Tori discuss whether to include Melissa in their group sleepover, and Melissa overhears at least part of their discussion. How does Melissa respond? What misunderstandings happen afterward on both sides because of that event? When Kate, Colt, and Tori discuss that they haven't seen Melissa since they first talked about the parade, what does Kate say? Tori? Colt? Who do you think has the best perspective to solve the issue, and why?

How could you use that perspective to clear up some tension you have in a relationship now, whether with someone you consider a friend or an enemy? How might you spread some "good gossip" instead of the gossip that divides and judges people?

Note from Kate

Colt was right. We should have come right out and asked Melissa if something was bothering her instead of talking behind her back. We weren't trying to be mean, but since she heard us talking, she didn't know that. I've decided I need to be careful about other people's feelings and try to put myself in their place instead of talking to a friend about them.

Secret #3

Have you faced any situation(s) where you felt "different" from the rest of a group? How were you treated as a result? How did that treatment make you feel about yourself? About others?

When Tori says that white kids sometimes treat her differently because she's Hispanic, how does Melissa respond? Do you think the others realize how being teased or ignored can affect someone else? Why or why not?

When have you treated someone as different and excluded her or him from your group? How can you become more like Kate, who didn't judge Tori but instead made friends with her?

Note from Kate

When I first moved to Odell, I sometimes felt like I was in the minority, as there were a lot more Hispanic kids there than at my old school. But I realized they are just kids, the same as me. They have dreams and hopes and things that have hurt them, and they don't want to be left out any more than I do. Tori and I are about as different as two people can be, but we're best friends. I'm so glad both of us looked past our skin color and decided to take a chance at being friends. I would have really missed out if we hadn't.

Secret #4

Have you ever met someone who has been the subject of gossip and has been misunderstood? How did you deal with it when people gossiped when you were around?

Mrs. Maynard's accident and her scar have caused her to stay in her home for long periods of time. As a result, some people think she's strange, and rumors were started about her to the point where she was even accused of burying someone on her property. This has caused Mrs. Maynard a lot of pain. Have you ever taken part in this kind of gossip that hurt someone else? Or have you had friends who gossiped about you? How did it affect your life? What might you do to change things?

Note from Kate

Tori, Colt, and I couldn't believe people could be so mean to Mrs. Maynard, and it made all of us mad. Then I realized that

Melissa's friends had done the same thing to her. In fact, we kind of did too. Melissa and Mrs. Maynard both felt left out and thrown away by their friends because they are different. Mrs. Maynard lost her beauty, and Melissa's family lost their money, but that didn't change who they are. When we finally figured that out, it made a big difference in understanding Melissa and Mrs. Maynard. From now on we're going to be more careful about judging people when we don't know their stories.

Kate and Tori's Chocolate Chip Coconut Oatmeal Cookies

These are the special cookies the girls made for Mrs. Maynard. You can have fun making them … and eating them too.

What you'll need:
  *1 cup butter, softened
  *1 cup sugar
  *1 cup brown sugar
  *2 eggs
  *2 teaspoons vanilla
  *2 cups flour (for flatter or softer cookies, use 1 1/2 cups
     of flour instead of 2 cups)
  *1 teaspoon baking soda
  *1 teaspoon baking powder
  *1/2 teaspoon salt
  *2 cups oats
  *1 cup shredded coconut

*1/2 cup chopped walnuts (if desired)

*Chocolate chips to taste

*Ungreased cookie sheet

1. Preheat oven to 325 degrees.

2. Combine butter, sugar, brown sugar, eggs, and vanilla in large mixing bowl.

3. Beat with mixer until fully blended.

4. Add remaining ingredients to blended mixture and mix with large spoon or mixer on low speed.

5. Place spoonfuls of batter on ungreased cookie sheet and bake 8–10 minutes at 325 degrees.

Author's Note

I've been an avid horse lover all of my life. I can't remember a time when I wasn't fascinated with the idea of owning a horse, although it didn't happen until after I married. My family lived in a small town on a couple of acres that were mostly steep hill-side, so other than our lawn and garden area, there was no room for a horse. I lived out my dreams by reading every book I could find that had anything to do with horses.

My first horse was a two-year-old Arabian gelding named Nicky, who taught me so much and caused me to fall deeply in love with the Arabian breed. Over the years we've owned a stallion, a number of mares, a handful of foals, and a couple of geldings. It didn't take too many years to discover I couldn't make money in breeding. After losing a mare and baby due to a reaction to penicillin, and having another mare reject her baby at birth, we decided it was time to leave that part of the horse industry and simply enjoy owning a riding horse or two.

Our daughter, Marnee, brought loving horses to a whole new level. She was begging to ride when she was two to three years old and was riding her own pony alone at age five. Within a few years, she requested lessons, as she wanted to switch from

Western trail riding to showing English, both in flat work and hunt-seat, and later, in basic dressage. I learned so much listening to her instructor and watching that I decided to take lessons myself.

We spent a couple of years in the show world, but Marnee soon discovered she wanted to learn for the sake of improving her own skills more than competing, and she became a first-rate horsewoman.

We still ride together, as she and her husband, Brian, own property next to ours. My old Arabian mare, Khaila, was my faithful trail horse for over seventeen years and lived with Marnee's horses on their property, so she wouldn't be lonely. At the age of twenty-six, she began having serious age-related problems and went on to horse heaven in late July of 2013. Now I ride Brian's Arabian mare, Sagar, when Marnee and I trail-ride. I am so blessed to have a daughter who shares the same love as me and to have had so many wonderful years exploring the countryside with my faithful horse Khaila.

If you don't own your own horse yet, don't give up. It might not happen while you still live at home, and you might have to live out your dreams in books, or even by taking a lesson at a local barn, but that's okay. God knows your desire and will help fulfill it in His perfect way.

Acknowledgments

This series has been a brand-new adventure for me—one I never expected, but one I'm so blessed to have experienced. I've loved horses all my life and owned them since I was nineteen, but I never thought I'd write horse novels for girls. I'm so glad I was wrong!

So many people have helped make this series possible: My friends at church, who were excited when I shared God's prompting and offered to pray that the project would find a home, as well as my family, my friends, and my critique group, who believed in me, listened, read my work, and cheered me on. There have also been a number of authors who helped me brainstorm ideas for the series or specific sections of one book or the other when I struggled—Kimberly, Vickie, Margaret, Cheryl, Lissa, Nancy—you've all been such a blessing!

My fan group and Street Team on Facebook helped me when I hit a wall in my story line. They eagerly brainstormed with me and came up with the idea of the kids riding in a parade. My editor, Ramona, suggested a way to tie the parade in with the *Mystery Rider*. Books are rarely written completely alone, and I'm so thankful for the help of friends and readers.

I also want to thank the team at David C Cook. I was so thrilled when Don Pape asked if I'd consider sending this series to him to review when I mentioned I was writing it. The horse lovers on the committee snatched it up and galloped with it, and I was so excited! I love working with this company and pray we'll have many more years and books together. Thank you to all who made this a possibility and, we pray, a resounding success!

You can learn more about me and all of my books at www.miraleeferrell.com. Thank you for taking the time to read my new series, and watch for another book in four months!

About the Author

Miralee Ferrell, the author of the Horses and Friends series plus twelve other novels, was always an avid reader. She started collecting first edition Zane Grey Westerns as a young teen. But she never felt the desire to write books ... until after she turned fifty. Inspired by Zane Grey and old Western movies, she decided to write stories set in the Old West in the 1880s.

After she wrote her first Western novel, *Love Finds You in Last Chance, California*, she was hooked. Her *Love Finds You in Sundance, Wyoming* won the Will Rogers Medallion Award for Western fiction, and Universal Studios requested a copy of her debut novel, *The Other Daughter*, for a potential family movie.

Miralee loves horseback riding on the wooded trails near her home with her married daughter, who lives nearby, and spending time with her granddaughter, Kate. Besides her horse friends, she's owned cats, dogs (a six-pound, long-haired Chihuahua named Lacey was often curled up on her lap as she wrote this book), rabbits, chickens, and even two cougars,

Spunky and Sierra, rescued from breeders who couldn't care for them properly.

Miralee would love to hear from you:

www.miraleeferrell.com (blog, newsletter, and website)
www.twitter.com/miraleeferrell
www.facebook.com/miraleeferrell
www.facebook.com/groups/82316202888 (fan group)

Sneak Peek at Book Four: Blue Ribbon Trail Ride

Chapter One

Upper Hood River Valley, Odell, Oregon
Summer, Present Day

Thirteen-year-old Kate Ferris and her best friend, Tori Velasquez, lay on a pile of loose hay in the loft above the stalls in the barn Kate's family owned. Kate rolled onto her stomach and propped herself on her elbows. "I love working here, but I'm glad the chores are done this early in the day. It's so hot."

Tori batted at a fly that tried to land on her face. "Yuck. I hate flies. It sure would be nice to go swimming, but the Hood River pool is too far."

"I know. I already asked Mom, and she said we'd have to wait until she's going to town. What do you want to do now? I don't feel like riding in this heat, even if we don't often have the arena to ourselves. Want to turn on the sprinkler and get cooled off?"

Tori sat up and opened her mouth to speak then shut it as Kate pointed below. Kate's parents walked across the arena and headed toward the office.

Kate peered over the edge. She lifted her hand and started to wave, but something about her mother's expression stopped her. Instead she placed her finger to her lips and shook her head at Tori. It wasn't that she wanted to spy on her parents, but something was up, and she'd like to know what. She scrambled to think of anything she might have done wrong, but nothing came to mind. They'd been helping Mrs. Maynard, an older neighbor up the road with her chores, and Kate had finished everything in the barn and house that Mom had asked, so that couldn't be what put a frown on her mother's face.

Mom paused outside the office door. "It makes me sick that we can't do it, John. That camp has such a great reputation for helping autistic kids, and it's amazing they still have openings. Isn't there any way we could swing it?"

"I'm sorry, Nan. I don't see how. This boarding stable pays its way almost every month, but the first two months it cost more than it brought in."

Kate's heart jolted. Mom and Dad weren't thinking of shutting it down, were they? She stared at Tori, who looked nervous. Her friend must be thinking the same thing. She leaned forward again, hoping that wasn't where this conversation was headed.

"I know. But we actually turned a profit last month. The horse show gave us excellent advertising."

"Which is great," Kate's dad said. "And as long as that continues, we'll keep it open. But we still don't have the extra it would take for Pete's camp. I'm sorry, honey. It's not in our budget for this summer, unless God gives us a miracle."

Kate's mom nodded. "Let's take one more look at the books, but I know you're right, John. It breaks my heart Pete can't go when it could be such a help in his progress."

Kate's dad opened the door to the office and let her mom go in first, then followed and shut it behind him.

Kate sucked in a breath. "Wow. I thought for sure they were going to say they were closing the barn."

Tori made a face. "Me too. I'm thankful they aren't, but I'm thinking about Pete. That camp sounds awesome."

"This is the first I've heard of it. I'm surprised Mom and Dad haven't said anything before."

"Maybe they didn't want to get Pete's hopes up. He might not say a lot, but he's a smart kid."

"I know." Kate thought for a moment. "How about we call Colt and Melissa and see if we can figure out a way to make enough money to send Pete to camp?"

Tori pushed to her knees, her brown eyes sparkling. "Cool! Let's go."

Kate followed Tori down the ladder to the lower level. "We'd better keep our voices down. Mom and Dad might think we were spying on them." She felt bad that she'd wanted to listen, and even worse that the first thing she'd thought about was losing the boarding stable, while Tori's first comment had been about Pete. But right now she was glad she'd been in the barn loft, or they'd never have known her family couldn't afford the camp. Somehow she and her friends had to find a way to make a difference.

A short while later Kate and her three friends sat in the shade of the towering fir tree in the backyard after cooling off in the sprinkler. Kate lifted a glass of lemonade and took a long drink, then set it on the small table near her lawn chair. "I'm glad you guys could come over and help us plan."

Colt, their thirteen-year-old friend who homeschooled and rode Western, switched a piece of straw to the other side of his mouth. "I've heard about that camp for autistic kids. Mom has a friend who was a cabin leader one year, and she told us how awesome it is. The kids all seem to love it. It's a bummer it costs so much."

Melissa, who'd once been the most popular girl in school, settled into a chair on the other side of Colt. "Your little brother is one of the sweetest kids I know, Kate. He deserves to go."

Tori nodded. "I agree. That's why we wanted the two of you to come help us figure out a way to raise money."

Kate leaned forward. "I've been thinking. Wouldn't it be great if we could put together some type of horse-related event that the entire community could take part in? And we could make autism the focus of the fund-raiser. Pete would benefit, but if we raised enough money, other kids might be able to go to camp too."

"Cool!" Colt grinned so wide he almost lost the straw from the corner of his lips, but he tucked it back in. "Anybody have any brilliant ideas of a horse event that would bring in serious money?"

Melissa flipped her blonde hair over her shoulder. "Well, if it's to benefit special kids like Pete, I'll bet a lot of the townspeople might get involved. What do you think about some kind of trail ride where people win prizes?"

Kate exhaled. "I love it. Way to go, Melissa." It never failed to surprise her how smart and kind Melissa had turned out to be, once she got over being stuck-up. A twinge of guilt hit Kate. That wasn't fair. Melissa hadn't been stuck-up as much as she'd been hurt in the past by friends who misjudged her and used her when they thought she was wealthy.

Sure, Melissa had been unkind to her and Tori in the beginning, but she later admitted a lot of it was because she was jealous of them. That had totally floored Kate. The popular, pretty girl jealous of them! But Melissa had envied Kate's family life, and now she understood why. Melissa's mom had allowed her divorce and loss of their money to push her to drink and yell at Melissa a lot. Since Kate, Tori, and Colt had accepted Melissa and taken her into their circle of friends, the girl had changed into someone they enjoyed having around.

Tori frowned. "I don't get it. How can a trail ride bring in money and let people win prizes? The prizes would cost us money, right? And wouldn't they have to be awfully big to make anyone want to pay to take part?"

"Actually, it's a great idea." Colt rubbed his chin. "When I lived in Montana, I went on a trail ride like that, but it was a scavenger hunt. The sponsors hid items along the trail. Participants were given clues and had to hunt for the items. There was a big prize at the end for the person who found the most items, but there were a lot of prizes for people who came in second and third—even riders who found all the items but didn't get there fast. We could do age categories to make it fair. We had a great turnout, and horse clubs from all over took part."

Tori waved her hand. "I still don't get it. How would we pay for the prizes? From the entry fee people pay?"

Kate shook her head. "Nope. All of that money goes into the fund. We go to businesses in Hood River, not just here in Odell. We ask them to donate gift certificates or items from their store as prizes, right, Colt?"

"Right. Some of the businesses donated really cool stuff. The barn that sponsored the ride took out ads in the paper. You know, the *Hood River News* would probably give us a free ad, since it's a fund-raiser."

Tori groaned. "So, let's see if I get this right. Who goes out and asks all these businesspeople and the newspaper to donate stuff?"

Melissa gave one of her old smirks. "We do, silly. But hey, it's not a big deal. I've done fund-raising with the Pony Club." She turned her head. "When I used to belong, I mean."

Kate's heart lurched at the pain in Melissa's voice. She'd wondered if Melissa had dropped out since they no longer had the money. "Great! Then you can be our expert and make sure we know what to say. You did an awesome job getting us organized for the parade."

"Seriously?" Melissa's voice squeaked. "You want me to be in charge again? Why?"

Kate smiled. "Because you're a natural leader, that's why."

"But I might mess it up. What if no one wants to give anything?" A note of panic crept into her words. "Some of the people in town knew my dad, and since he left ..."

Tori reached her hand out and grabbed Melissa's. "That's not going to happen, Melissa. Like Kate said, you're good at this stuff, and we trust you. Nothing's going to go wrong. Just you wait and see."

Books by Miralee Ferrell

Horses and Friends Series
A Horse for Kate
Silver Spurs
Mystery Rider

Love Blossoms in Oregon Series
Blowing on Dandelions
Forget Me Not
Wishing on Buttercups
Dreaming on Daisies

The 12 Brides of Christmas Series
The Nativity Bride

The 12 Brides of Summer Series
The Dogwood Blossom Bride

Love Finds You Series
Love Finds You in Bridal Veil, Oregon
Recently republished as *Finding Love in Bridal Veil, Oregon*
Love Finds You in Sundance, Wyoming
Love Finds You in Last Chance, California
Love Finds You in Tombstone, Arizona
(sequel to *Love Finds You in Last Chance, California*)
Recently republished as *Finding Love in Tombstone, Arizona*
The Other Daughter
Finding Jeena
(sequel to *The Other Daughter*)

Other Contributions/Compilations
A Cup of Comfort for Cat Lovers
Fighting Fear: Winning the War at Home
Faith & Finances: In God We Trust
Faith & Family: A Christian Living Daily
Devotional for Parents and Their Kids

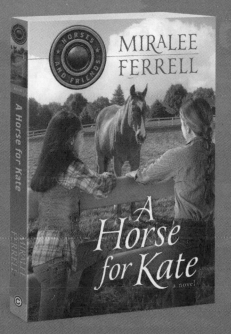

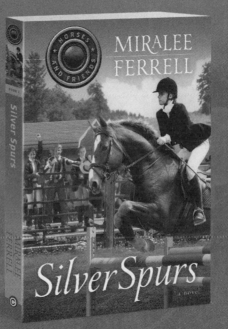

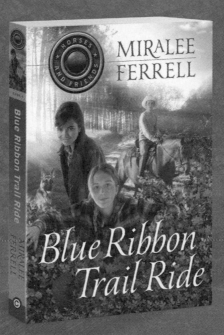